Postcards from
BABEL

a satirical novel

Jill Hadfield

Olive Press

First published in Great Britain 1990
by Olive Press, 112 Bolingbroke Grove, London SW11 1DA

ISBN 0 946889 21 X

Typeset by Photoprint, Torquay, Devon.
Printed in Great Britain by
Billing & Sons Ltd, Worcester

There is no such thing as society.
Margaret Thatcher

Nel mezzo del cammin di nostra vita
Mi ritrovai per una selva oscura
Che la diritta via era smarrita.
Dante, *Inferno.*

For Charlie

The Ground Floor

Babel, 19 May 1999

Well, it's not quite as I imagined! Very imposing, of course, the world's largest building: this huge white tower, fifty miles across and five miles high. But the strangest thing is the silence! I'd imagined it full of noise and bustle with colourful characters chattering away in their incomprehensible languages. My first impressions, though, are of long white corridors leading in all directions, and this deathly hush everywhere.

The official Inlinguist guide who met us at the airport said it used to be just as I imagined it until the Minimize Discord policy came in in the late eighties and the sealed concept module was developed. According to the government handbook for tourists that we were issued with: 'The lexical differentiation factor between concept groups became alarmingly high in the early nineties. Accordingly, different concept groups were allocated their own sealed modules to optimize agreement potential and minimize negative interaction due to miscomprehension interfacing.'

Babble is the official language here. I only studied it up to fifth form in school and it's getting a little rusty now, so I had some trouble understanding this, and asked my guide to translate. 'It's very simple,' she said. 'Everyone had different ideas and they all used to argue a lot. But they all spoke different languages, so they didn't understand each other. This only made them argue worse, and the more they argued and the more ideas they had, the more different their languages became. Things really were getting quite violent until our Beloved Leader came up with the Sealed Concept Module policy.'

I had heard this phrase a few times by now, so I asked her

to explain it. 'You'll see when we go on the tour tomorrow,' she said, 'but basically we restructured the tower so that different language groups now live in separate areas called concept modules. Now there is no arguing and everyone can agree happily in the same language.' I dimly recalled hearing about this in history lessons at school, so I said, 'Oh yes, isn't that called the Divide and Survive policy?' My guide's face went quite white and she looked around as if to see if anyone had overheard. I had obviously unwittingly upset her, for her manner changed completely. 'Certainly not,' she said primly. 'We call it Bringing Harmony Where There Was Discord. Now if you care to go to the dining-room, I think you'll find it is time for supper.'

I met a very interesting and varied group of people at supper. I sat next to Rick, a lean and rangy Australian who is very well travelled and kept us entertained with anecdotes about his various trips, and Klaus, an earnest German art historian, who is extremely knowledgeable on the subject of Babel architecture. Then there was Johnny, an ageing flowerchild from Boulder, Colorado, who wears faded denims and a fringed jacket, and Dorothy, a crimplene-suited matron in her mid-fifties, who goes in for matching shoes and bags. I got on best with Tracey and Miranda, two friends who work in the same office – although they couldn't be more different. Miranda has long brown hair and round brown eyes and wears hair ribbons and dresses with puffed sleeves and sashes, whereas Tracey's style involves low necklines and a lot of mascara. They have what I consider a sensible attitude to travel: they told me that they've been saving for a long time for this trip and are determined to make the most of every single minute. There were three rather silent members of the group. Hugo and Rosamund, a pair of newly-weds who are honeymooning here in Babel, hardly said a word to the rest of us and spent most of the meal gazing into each other's eyes. It was very touching to see them. The only member of the group whom I took an active dislike to was a rather gloomy-looking and taciturn Italian, who sat at the far end of the table. He made no attempt to join in the conversation, but sat there looking melancholy and sensitive, occasionally scribbling things in a little notebook. When he had finished eating, he simply got up and left with no more than a curt nod to us.

After supper, Klaus, Rick and I went for a little walk before turning in. I found Babel scenery pretty monotonous, I must say – nothing but white walls and white carpet everywhere you look – and Rick said that it was not a patch on India or Thailand, but Klaus said that first appearances were deceptive, and in the week to come we would find a plethora of architectural styles illustrative of every period in Babel history. He actually said a good deal more on the subject, but I found it a little difficult to concentrate after the first couple of paragraphs. We wandered down the corridor for a mile or so and came to a huge barred door guarded by sentries. We asked if we could go in, but apparently it's impossible to enter any concept module unless you have a government validated entry permit and are accompanied by an official Inlinguist interpreter and Discord Minimizer. But no doubt we'll be taken there on the tour tomorrow.

Babel, 20 May 1999

What an interesting day! And what a wonderful place this is! There's so much variety and local colour, and yet the whole society is run so smoothly. It really is most impressive.

After breakfast, our guide explained to us how the tour will be arranged. We will be working our way slowly up the tower, visiting different modules on the way and stopping on different floors overnight to give us a chance to take in the distinctive local atmosphere and sample the local cuisine.

We started here on the Ground Floor at the huge barred door I told you about yesterday. Our guide handed over a sheaf of official documents. The sentries checked these carefully, searched our bags for offensive weapons or foreign literature, then pressed a button in the wall. The great door swung back and we were admitted.

Inside it was most picturesque. A maze of narrow streets led away from the door. The little red-brick houses were adorned with lace curtains at the windows and the front doorsteps were decorated with milk bottles and dustbins. Cars were parked all the way down the street, but I saw no one driving. Nor did I see any pedestrians. Miranda and I thought the houses were delightful, but Klaus said the style was rather aggressively mediocre.

After we had walked a couple of miles (with the guide pointing out landmarks like the Smedways Kiwifruit and Pernod Flavour Icecream Factory or the Foldaway Bedside Table with Built-in Video Sex Manual Production Unit), I decided to ask her why there was no one around in the streets. 'From the eighties onwards thoroughfare frequentation became less experientially significant,' she said, 'and now it is completely out-moded.'

'What do people do instead?' I asked. 'Modular dwellings are accessed to experience via their Facility Interfaces. This tour includes a visit to a dwelling, so you will see for yourself later, but just now, I'd like to direct your attention to the Calculator Wristwatch with Clip-on Compact Disc Player Factory.'

After lunch (taken in The Works Canteen, a nostalgia theme pub where we ate Microwave Pasties with Brown Sauce and Crinkle-cut Chips – our guide assured us that all the details were absolutely authentic down to the formica tables and sauce bottles), we had the opportunity to enter some dwellings and see the local customs and folklore for ourselves at first hand.

The little homes were really quite comfortable and very colourful, with brightly patterned carpets and flowery wallpaper and as our guide pointed out, although they seemed similar from the outside, inside each was quite choice-individualized and discrimination-differentiated. In one, for example, the kitchen units were in Mulberry and Cabbage and the owner had chosen a Toastofast Microwave Toaster with Automatic Slicer and Butterer, whereas the dwelling next door had a kitchen decorated in Nectarine and Avocado, and the owner had gone for a Nuclear-Powered Barbecue Unit with Automatic Calorie-Counter.

But I was most impressed by the Facility Interface. This was a large machine that took up most of the living area. In each dwelling the family (or modular unit as I am learning to call them) were seated in a row in front of the interface. Each member was connected to the interface via headphones and special glasses. To an outside observer it didn't seem as if much was happening. Occasionally a unit member would press one of a row of buttons inlaid in the arm of their chair and lights would blink on the machine. Sometimes a trapdoor would open in the floor and a small Stowaway Interface Snack Table would appear with a can of Uglifruit and Bilberry Fizzy Drink or a packet of Smoked Mackerel and Peanut Butter Crisps, or a parcel would arrive through a chute built into the wall.

I asked what these parcels contained and our guide said they were probably the week's shopping or a new Housework Alleviation Device, but might be a Homecare Product such as an Aerosol Tudor Rose EasiStencil Kit for Patterning Bath, Basin and Lavatory Bowl or a Child's Play Facilitator such as the latest Videoporn Game or Dismember Your Own

Horrordoll Kit. Through the Facility Interface, she explained, the unit is not only accessed into a whole range of Leisure Viewplay and Fantasy Actualization activities, but can also activate consumer choices.

'But do people never go to the shops?' I asked. 'In the early nineties,' my guide explained patiently, 'it was realized that shopping was a non-viable leisure activity: the inconvenience factor was simply too high. The shop as a recreational concept ceased to exist and we built a Consumer Selector and Dispenser Device into the interface. So, at a stroke, we have done away with the need for driving, parking, walking and carrying. All activities are now dwelling-centred.' 'What about work?' I asked. 'Don't people need to go outside to work? What about all those factories we saw this morning?' 'Since Total Automatization came in in the nineties,' she said happily, 'the need for on-site effort has been totally eradicated. The emphasis has been shifted from production to production overseeing, which can be completely push-button effectuated and dwelling-based.' 'Through the Facility Interface?' 'Through the Facility Interface.'

I looked with new respect at this wonderful machine. 'But aren't there a lot of arguments?' I asked, remembering acrimonious discussions in my own family. Our guide looked puzzled. 'Don't the family, sorry modular unit, ever argue over which channel to watch?' Her face cleared. 'Oh no, the necessity for that never arises. The Channel Individualization Feature built into spectacles and headphones eliminates the need for communal viewing. Besides, the units in this module are highly developed and have evolved out of disagreement mode since they have voluntarily discarded their language actuation ability.' I was shocked at first. 'Do you mean they can't communicate?' I stuttered. 'Then how can they understand the Facility Interface?' By now, the guide was becoming a little annoyed at my obtuseness. 'They still function linguistically in receptive mode, of course,' she said impatiently. 'That's necessary for survival. They have just evolved out of the necessity for active mode.' Do you mean they can understand but not speak?' She nodded her head testily. 'But that would mean that they can't discuss . . . She continued for me, '. . . argue, quarrel, fight, swear or abuse each other. The atrophy of the expression function has indeed led to a more harmonious and less discordant society. See how happy they look.'

I looked at the family in front of me. Their faces were so obscured by gadgetry that it was difficult to make out their exact expressions. However, they didn't look unhappy. 'So do they never go out at all?' I asked. 'Does everyone spend all day interfacing?' 'The interface indeed obviates the necessity for external environmental experience,' she agreed, 'and units are increasingly feeling less and less need for external venture since the experience potential offered by the interface is much richer than that offered by external reality.' 'Why go out when you can have all your fantasies realized in the privacy of your home?' 'Exactly,' she agreed.

'However, units do sometimes externalize their nostalgia needs and feel the desire to experience an out-moded pleasure form.' 'Such as?' 'Units may sometimes feel the need to go for a Sunday drive. Cars are no longer necessary, of course, since no one needs to go anywhere. However, they are an essential part of Consumer Purchasing, and sometimes units feel the need to play with them. Alternatively, unit heads sometimes feel the desire to go to the pub on Friday nights. This desire is obviously nostalgia-originated and we have tried to decorate the pubs accordingly – for example, the one you saw today.' 'But don't people go to the pub in order to talk?' She threw me a withering glance. 'People aren't *that* nostalgic. That went out before most of them were born. No, they go to operate the computer games and pinball machines – they have much more sophisticated viewplay facilities on the interface of course, but as I said, it's a kind of hankering after the past. But over recent years there has been a continuing downward trend in the number of pubvisitations per dwelling, and this can only be a healthy sign that unit members are finding contentment and harmony within the bosom of their families, for as our dear Leader said: 'The Family is the Building Block of Society.'

I followed her eyes upward to where a framed text on the mantlepiece above the Magiglow Real Woodsmoke Effect Log Fire said: 'The basic ties of the family are at the heart of society and very nursery of civic virtue.' If only our own quarrelsome society could be founded on precepts like these!

Babel, 20 May, evening

As we were walking back to the hotel I realized that something had been worrying me vaguely, so I asked our guide about it. 'But what would happen, say, if someone, a unit member I mean, decided they didn't want to stay indoors or didn't like the Facility Interface? Is it forbidden to go out just to walk around?' 'Of course not!' said our guide, laughing. 'This is a free society you know. It's just that Streetlife is a different concept module entirely. I can take you there if you like – it's only a short walk away. After dinner might be a good time – the nightlife is quite exciting.'

Some of the group felt rather tired and decided to stay in and watch the latest Fantasmoporn on the hotel interface, but after dinner (Italian Peasant Style Deep Fried Lasagne Croquettes followed by Crunchifri Breadcrumbed Texan Apple Pancake Fritters), Rick and Klaus and I elected to go on the trip and eventually Miranda said she would join us. She was feeling somewhat abandoned as Tracey had an assignment with Johnny, or John the Baptist, as Dorothy has christened him; something to do with his flowing hair and glazed expression, I suppose. We walked down the corridor to the next barred door. 'What's on tonight, Bill?' asked our guide as the sentry issued us with our protective headgear and bodyshields. 'Well, the main game is Skins United versus The Angels, but there's a good bit of mugging going on at the far end of the stadium and you might also catch the tail end of the eight o'clock riot if you hurry.'

We queued up for tickets for the game and then entered the module. What a different world! The colour, the noise and the bustle took my breath away, and I stood entranced at the sheer spectacle. Such variety, such colour and life! Near us a group of young people dressed in glossy black leather gaily decorated with silver studs were having the time of their lives kicking someone's head in, while other youngsters with closely shaven heads were playing an energetic game of Grab the Money and Run or Bash the Pensioner. Colourful characters in gorgeous tribal costume with painted faces and bright green or purple hair were grappling merrily with each other, and at the far end of the street the bright lights of petrol bombs arced through the darkness. The heady scent of tear gas was in the air and the night was alive with the yell of obscenities and the wail of police sirens. We found it hard to tear ourselves away from this fascinating place, but our guide pointed out that the main game was starting soon in the stadium and we'd better hurry if we wanted to be sure of a place.

We were just in time. As we wriggled into our places on the stand, the teams trooped in to roars of acclamation from the crowd. It took some time for them all to get into position as each team was several hundred strong, and as they stood there eyeing each other up and waiting for the referee's whistle, I tried to remember the rules of the game as I had learned it in Customs and Sports of Other Cultures at school. It struck me that one thing was missing. 'Where's the ball?' I whispered to the guide. 'Ball?' she queried. 'You know – the thing they kick around the pitch.' 'Oh, they'll soon find one,' she said. 'But look, they're going to begin.'

There was an expectant hush. The referee blew his whistle and the game began. Both sides ran eagerly towards the centre of the pitch and for a few minutes all you could see was a confused tangle of black leather, boots, studs and braces as they joined in the scrum. The crowd was roaring its appreciation. 'Put the boot in!' 'Do him in!' 'Knee him in the balls!' they shouted enthusiastically.

Suddenly a shaven head emerged from the scrum. It was being kicked towards the United goalpost. Two Skins ran to tackle. There was a muffled explosion and the Angel centre forward fell flat on his face. The referee blew his whistle and ran forward. The crowd was yelling, 'Foul, foul!' 'Why was that a foul?' I asked the guide. Her attention was on the pitch where the offending Skin was being removed by a detachment of police in armoured cars. 'Using a gun,' she replied briefly. 'Only chains and flick knives allowed.'

My attention was temporarily diverted from the pitch by a minor scuffle to my right, where two United supporters were quietly stabbing a tall youth in the Angel colours of black and silver, so I didn't see the moment when the head was actually kicked into the goal, but the crowd went wild in a frenzy of joy and exhilaration and several more Angel supporters were hacked to pieces in the excitement. The game lasted over an hour and the final score was 345 – 423 to the Angels. I was enthralled throughout by the colour and vivacity of the spectacle. Miranda thought it was one of the most exciting evenings she had had for a long time, but Rick said that if we liked that kind of thing we really ought to go to a Thai boxing match sometime. I was only sorry that the game had ended so soon and we had to make our way back to the hotel.

But the evening wasn't over yet. As we wandered back through the streets, where a few last partygoers were beating each other up in doorways, the windows rattled and the houses shook to the shock of a huge explosion. 'What was that?' I asked, momentarily taken aback. 'Oh, that probably came from the Terrorist Annexe,' said our guide, shaking brick dust and glass splinters from her hair. 'Would you like to see it?' 'It sounds a bit dangerous,' I said, recalling what I had learned about terrorism in World Politics: Factions and Fanatics in school. 'Not really,' said the guide, 'we can go in an armoured car. And the best time to go is usually just after an explosion. After they've had one, they usually spend some time working up towards the next one.'

So we collected a permit from the sentry and sped off down the corridor to the Annexe, a complex of low buildings and concrete bunkers built onto the side of the tower. It was rather a disappointment to me actually. I'd expected at least as much colour and life as in the Streetlife section, but this was all rather gloomy and not much fun at all. It all seemed desperately serious. We wandered through a rabbit warren of grimy and dimly lit rooms, where various shabby and intense looking characters were muttering darkly in corners or fiddling with complicated equipment involving lots of wires and suitcases. And I didn't understand much of what the local guide was saying.

'This group here,' he informed us, 'is dedicated to the overthrow of the cryptofascist neoimperialist counter-revolutionaries in Birmingham North and this cell here is working for the liberation of Manchester from the iron grip of bourgeois reactionaries masquerading as liberal democrats.'

All this verbiage seemed a far cry from the spontaneous expressions of enthusiasm in the module we had just visited. 'This is the Theory and Advance Planning section,' our guide whispered as the local guide mumbled on into his beard about the liberation of the proletarian masses of Hampstead from their domination by cryptoimperialist reactionary neofascist bourgeois intellectuals, 'the Practice section is outside.' 'Can we see it?' I asked, hoping for something a bit livelier. 'As I said, I don't think there'll be anything on. But we can ask Rudi.' Rudi consulted a large timetable. 'No, nothing else planned for tonight. But there's a hijack scheduled for tomorrow evening.' 'Oh, what a shame, by then we'll be on the Third Floor,' said our guide. Thanking him politely for his time and attention, and hoping the hijack would go without any hitches, she led us towards the exit.

As we waited for the security guard to validate our exit permits, I noticed a small door in the wall. The door was tightly bolted and barred with massive planks of wood. It had an air of neglect. Dusty cobwebs hung around the hinges and the padlocks were seized up with rust. Yet it seemed to me that I could hear sounds like muffled cries of pain. I peered at it. A barely decipherable sign in peeling white paint said: ULCER. 'What happens in there?' I asked the guide. She gave the door a quick glance. 'Oh, it's some kind of family quarrel that no one understands,' she said. 'I don't know what's going on there now – the door's been locked for years. They used to cause a terrible fuss and get in everyone's way, but people eventually gave up trying to understand them, so they simply shut the door on them and left them to their own devices. No one's been in there for years.'

Walking back to the hotel down the white-walled corridor, something occurred to me and I decided to ask the guide. 'You said that the key policy of the Babel government was putting a stop to disagreement.' 'Minimizing Discord, yes,' she corrected me. 'Well, in those two modules we just visited, it was lively, but it wasn't exactly harmonious. Weren't they disagreeing?' 'Yes,' she explained, 'but they were disagreeing in the *same language*.' I must have looked confused, for she went on, 'Disagreement is their mode. It's their reality-interface. We live in a perfectly free society, so they have to be allowed to express themselves. This caused a problem in the old days when they disagreed with people who didn't understand them and lifestyle-impingement took place. That's the beauty of the sealed module concept: now they have perfect freedom of self-expression in their own linguistic modes, and lifestyle-impingement on other linguistic groups has been eradicated. Of course these modules are perhaps temporarily falling a little short of the ideals of the sanctity of life and the responsibility that comes with freedom, on which our society is founded, but the problem will be solved in time by a natural process of modular self-elimination.' 'Modular self-elimination?' Perhaps my incessant questions were beginning to annoy her, perhaps the lateness of the hour was finally beginning to tell on her, for she responded rather brusquely and in a manner quite unlike her usual elegant speech. She slipped for a moment into Streetspeak, 'Yeah, lock the buggers up where they can't get in anyone's way and let them all blow each other up.'

Babel, 21 May 1999

What an interesting day! This is one of the most fascinating and varied countries I have ever visited! Today I had a rather unexpected adventure, which gave me a glimpse into a completely different way of life and enabled me to see some quaint and charming folk customs at first hand.

This morning we were at leisure in our hotel, and many of the group decided to watch a documentary, *Secret Confessions of the Royal Bedchamber*, on the interface, but as the day was bright and sunny, a few of us decided to go for a stroll. Our guide very kindly gave up her free morning to accompany us. As she said, we might get lost and be unable to find the way back to the hotel – and who would there be to give us directions?

We began our walk with a stroll among the factories. I was with Klaus, who really is extremely informative. The only trouble is, I seem to have forgotten a lot of what he was saying. I must bring a notebook next time. I was so busy listening that I didn't have much time to look around me, but I did notice one curious thing that had escaped my attention yesterday: many of the factories we passed had an abandoned and derelict air. When I pointed this out, our guide (I'm not quite sure of her name, by the way: I thought it was Virginia, but when she pronounces it, it sounds like Virgilia – I find it very difficult to distinguish between 'l' and 'n' in Babble) explained that due to a variety of factors such as machinery-streamlining, productioncost-minimizing, wage-cutting, cost-efficiency, product-obsolescence and lucrative-takeoverbids, occasionally factories found that it was in the customers' and workers' interest to rationalize the workforce.

'Don't the workers ever go on strike?' I asked. She didn't seem to understand the word, so again I had to explain. The Babble I learnt at school is decidedly out-of-date! Even when she understood the word, she still looked puzzled. 'But what would there be to protest about?' she asked. 'They know that rationalization is in their own interests, to build a stronger country, to stimulate the economy, encourage initiative and personal responsibility, and to secure a better life for their children, and that they will be the winners in the long run.

They know that there simply is no alternative. Besides, how could they protest?' I saw her point.

I was about to ask what happened to rationalized workers, when my attention was distracted by the sight of the Smedways Kiwifruit and Pernod Flavour Icecream Factory that we had seen on the tour yesterday. The Smedways sign had been removed and had been replaced by another, which read, in bright neon lights: SMEDFIELDS KIWIFRUIT AND BILBERRY ICECREAM AND FIZZY DRINK COMPANY. 'What's happened there?' I asked Virgilia. Before she had time to answer, the neon letters went out, blinked erratically for a few seconds and then rearranged themselves to spell out a new name: MACSMEDFIELDS FOLDAWAY BEDSIDE TABLES WITH BUILT-IN VIDEO SEX MANUAL AND ICECREAM AND FIZZY DRINK DISPENSER. 'Oh, that's just a routine merger,' said Virgilia vaguely. 'Nothing to worry about; it happens all the time. I think we ought to be getting back to the hotel now, don't you?'

But as we turned to go back down the street, we encountered a long procession of men, women and children, suitcases in hand, bags and bundles on their backs, shuffling slowly towards the entrance. 'Are they going on holiday?' I asked. 'In a manner of speaking,' said Virgilia. As they passed the Macsmedfields factory several of the men turned their heads and spat. 'A quaint local custom,' explained Virgilia, 'a way of wishing good luck to the new management.'

New questions popped into my mind. 'Have they been rationalized? Where are they being taken?' 'They're not being *taken* anywhere,' said Virgilia, a trifle crossly. 'You do have some strange ideas. They have made conscious, free and responsible individual decisions to choose rationalization. You must remember that in Babel intervention by the State is never allowed to remove personal responsibility. Every individual is free to choose his or her personal lifemode, and the responsibility for that decision rests with the individual. Even if those in Government think the individual has made an unwise decision, they cannot influence an individual's lifemode-choice. That would be totalitarianism and we in Babel have a society dedicated to the ideals of freedom, democracy and individual choice.' Her eyes were bright and her cheeks were quite flushed after this stirring speech. I found her idealism and patriotism quite moving and unexpectedly I found tears coming into my eyes.

But I was still curious as to the destination of the rationalized workers. 'So where have they all chosen to go?' I asked. Virgilia sighed heavily. 'When a worker decides that the Ground Floor lifemode is, in his individual case, not entirely aspiration-compatible and selects the rationalization option, then he applies for rationalization pay and a transfer to the Basement.'

We had now reached the entry door where a rather touching farewell ceremony was taking place. Each worker, on leaving the door, was being presented with a small brown envelope and a sheaf of official-looking forms. I was by now very curious to see the place that so many people were choosing in preference to what seemed to me to be the blissful comfort of Ground Floor life, and so I pleaded with Virgilia to take us for a quick tour of the Basement. She was adamant, however. 'I'm afraid we haven't got time. The lift leaves for the Third Floor in half an hour, and since it wasn't on your tour agenda, it would take me a while to get the necessary permits.' She smiled at me kindly. 'You'll just have to come back to Babel another time – there's really too much to take in for one visit.'

But my curiosity about this basement wonderland had really been aroused and I must confess that I did something rather unorthodox. I followed the others into the hotel lobby, but under the pretext that I wanted to buy a Souvenir of Babel Glow-in-the-Dark Fluorescent T-shirt in the hotel shop, I detached myself from Dorothy, who was telling me about her gall bladder operation, slipped out again and joined the queue at the door. By pretending I was attached to the unit in front of me, I managed to avoid being questioned by the official giving out the forms, and I followed the line down the corridor and into the lift. I wanted so much to talk to the natives, to ask them about their feelings on leaving their homeland and how it felt to be rationalized and their reasons for choosing emigration when life on the Ground Floor seemed so comfortable, but attempts at communication were fruitless because of the language barrier.

The lift swished to a halt and we all marched out and filed along the corridor to where two sentries stood at an imposing gateway. Above the gateway a motto was emblazoned in flashing neon letters. It looked as if some of the letters had fallen off, but it was still possible to read the sign which said:

ABAN   ON   P   A   Y   WH   EN   HERE.

As we approached the gate, something rather odd happened. I felt a tap on my shoulder and, turning round, I saw a very old man. 'You're from the tour group aren't you?' he said. I was so taken aback to find someone not only speaking, but speaking my language, that I was speechless for a few moments. 'Oh yes,' he said, reading my thoughts, 'I haven't forgotten how to speak. I remember my education, you see.' 'But how do you speak my language?' I stammered. 'Did you learn it at school?' 'No, everyone used to speak it, or at least understand it. Books used to be written in it. That was in the days before linguistic diversification and dialect groups when Babble became the official language.' He sighed sadly. I wanted to ask more, but he went on, 'I just wanted to warn you. Don't go in there – not even for a look. If you go in you'll never come out again.'

I wanted to ask what he meant, but the sentries were pushing people forward, and he had disappeared in the crowd. I had now reached the gateway, which was wide and open, unlike the other heavily barricaded doors I had seen, and a sentry was asking me a question. 'You be for tea?' he enquired, in a charming rustic accent. I declined his kind offer, explaining that I had only just had breakfast, but to my surprise he became quite irritable and started waving a sheaf of pink forms in my face. I tried to tell him that I hadn't got any documents because I was only a tourist and all I wanted was a quick glance at the Basement before my lift took off for the Third Floor, but he shrugged his shoulders and pushed me in anyway.

My first reaction was alarm, as I remembered the old man's words, but this quickly turned to amazement as I surveyed the scene before me. Directly in front of me was an expanse of ground covered with a profusion of yellow flowers, tall grasses, cigarette ends, old tin cans, rusting machinery and plastic bags of various types. Beyond this lawn was an array of imposing-looking buildings, their grey walls gaily decorated with slogans and pictures in silver, green and black, their concrete colonnades opening onto endless vistas of broad and windswept concrete piazzas. I marvelled at the intricate construction: balconies ran the length of the buildings on all floors and these were connected by flights of stairs and walkways which ran between buildings and between levels in all directions and at all angles, rather like an elaborate motorway interchange for pedestrians.

Stretching from the gateway, as far as the eye could see, was a queue of people, the line snaking across piazzas and through colonnades, along wide boulevards and over wasteground, through overgrown playgrounds, across deserted shopping plazas, along balconies, up and down flights of stairs, backwards and forwards along the walkways and in and out of rooms. Old men were hobbling along, scarcely able to move, pimply young men with pale faces slouched along behind them, aged grannies struggled up the steps, pregnant women dragged bawling snot-nosed kids past disused playareas, greying or balding men stood in line looking about them with a bewildered and incredulous expression, young women in aprons and curlers pushed babies in perambulators or older women in wheelchairs – all of human life was there, it seemed!

I was so completely lost in contemplation of the scene that I didn't notice that I had been propelled forward by the motion of the crowd. I looked around me in panic, but couldn't see the gateway anywhere. There was no recognizable landmark. Grey walls surrounded me on all sides, grey walkways ran ahead and behind and above me, looping and intertwining over my head, on either side were boarded-up or shattered windows and closed doors. I had no idea which way to go.

In front of me the queue disappeared into a doorway and then curled out again. I pushed past the people in front, apologizing for jumping the queue. No one spoke, no one so much as looked at me, wrapped in their own meditative silence. I made my way through the door, which was labelled M326, and entered the room.

Inside, the same heavy silence prevailed. Rows of benches filled the room and on these the people sat, their faces as blank and impassive as the grey walls around them. At the far end of the room was a computer, and in front of its green screen sat a man. From time to time questions would flash onto the screen and the man would key in a message in reply. At length the machine began to wheeze and rattle, and produced from its innards a long green form. The man took this, got up and slowly made his way to the end of the queue that wound out of the door.

I seized my opportunity and sat down in front of the machine. 'What is your Personal Identity Code?' asked the machine. 'I haven't got one,' I typed in in reply. 'I am a tourist and . . . ' But before I could finish, the machine interrupted, 'Aliens without Identity Codes are required to report at F408 to fill in Registration Form 2358C before proceeding with further formalities.' 'I don't want to proceed with formalities,' I typed in furiously. 'I want to get out.' The machine grumbled to itself for a few minutes while I fidgeted nervously waiting for an answer. The answer, when it came, took me by surprise. 'To get out you will need a bike,' it said. 'I haven't got a bike here,' I typed. The answer this time was instantaneous. 'Then you can't get out,' it said. 'Please go to room F408 to fill in Registration Form 2358C.'

I was beginning to dislike this machine intensely, but I refused to give up. 'Where can I get a bike?' I typed. The machine wheezed and grumbled for a bit. It seemed to be searching through its files. Finally it produced an answer. 'Take the green Declaration Form 450X, the yellow Certificate 297V, Bicycle Application Form 839M and the Mean Test and proceed to J603,' it advised. The printer disgorged several vari-coloured sheets of paper. 'Thank you,' I typed. The machine seemed rather surprised. 'Don't mention it,' it said. 'Next candidate please.'

I sat down on a bench and studied the forms. The green one was headed: 'Declaration of Willingness to Accept Any Employment'. The yellow one was headed: 'Certificate of Ability to Cycle Distances Up To and Including 600 Miles'. Form 839M came in triplicate and contained questions about my eyesight, my ability to cycle in straight lines and previous convictions for cycling offences. The Mean Test was a single white sheet of paper containing two questions: 'Can you produce documentary evidence of your ability to support yourself financially unaided while travelling until such time as you enter into gainful employment?' and 'Can you pay cash down for the bike?'

I filled in the first three, but when I came to the Mean Test, a horrible realization took hold of me. I had left my wallet and traveller's cheques in my hotel room. I decided I had no other option but to try and find J603 anyway. Perhaps the machine there would be more understanding.

It took me some time to find J603. I pushed my way past the barely moving queue, raced up flights of steps, along balconies, down walkways. There were no signposts anywhere and there didn't seem to be much logic to the numbering. N786 was next to B351 and opposite L42. Perspective played strange tricks with angles and straight lines and several times I found myself going back along a corridor I had walked down a few minutes before. The queuers, however, all seemed to know where they were going, moving in a slow, steady, purposeful flow in and out of rooms and along walkways. There seemed to be no end to the line of people.

After some hours I found J603, a small room at the end of a flight of steps apparently going nowhere. The room was empty, except for the computer. I sat down with a sigh of relief. 'At last!' I typed triumphantly. 'I was beginning to think you didn't exist!' 'Perhaps you're right,' replied the machine cryptically. 'Have you completed the requisite forms?' I handed them over. It shuffled through them, sighing softly for a while. 'You have no money, correct?' it accused. 'I have no money here,' I typed, 'but . . . ' 'Then you can't have a bicycle. Please proceed to room F408 to register.' I remembered what had worked before. 'Where can I get money?' I typed. The machine bleeped and gurgled. 'To get money you need a job,' it replied. 'I'd like a job then,' I typed. 'You can't get a job here,' said the machine. 'Where can I get a job?' I typed. 'You have to get out to get a job,' said the machine. With a sinking feeling, I typed, 'How do I get out?' The machine bleeped wickedly. 'To get out you need a bike.'

Feeling near to despair, I typed, 'Please help me. What shall I do?' 'Certainly,' replied the machine courteously, 'I am here to help you. First you will need to proceed to room F408 in order to complete Aliens' Form . . .'

I didn't wait to read the rest. Almost sobbing with frustration, I got up to go. But before I left, some angry impulse made me type in, sarcastically, 'Thank you for your help.' As I stood up, the computer's green eye blinked several times very rapidly. It seemed to be having some kind of internal argument. Then a message suddenly flashed up on the screen. 'Don't go,' it said. Then, 'Stay and talk to me.' Surprised, I sat down again. The machine spluttered a little. Then a flood of words poured out onto the screen. 'No one has ever said thank you to me before,' it said. 'You can't imagine what this means to me.' Puzzled, I read on. 'You mustn't get the wrong idea,' the machine went on, the words spilling furiously onto the screen from some hidden databank, 'I'm not really like this.'

'Like what?' I typed in. 'So cold and unfeeling,' said the machine. 'It's not that I don't want to help you get out. I do. I'd like to help everyone get out. But I can't help my programming. I have to obey the system. It's not my fault.' 'Then whose fault is it?' I typed in. 'Who programmes you? Who is responsible for creating the system?' The machine sobbed gently. It seemed to be having trouble collecting itself. Then a sentence unfolded itself slowly and painfully. The ill-formed letters read: 'THe lady of THe CelestiAl RosE'.

'Who is she?' I asked, mystified. An attack of hiccups seized the machine. Letters began appearing, jerkily and at random, until the screen was filled with a mass of Cs, Hs, Ts and Rs. Then in a sudden frenzy it began to print out a document. But after a few lines the printer stopped dead. The green screen flashed once, then faded. I watched, wondering what was happening. Then a message appeared on the screen: ERROR IN DATA INPUT, it said. Then: THIS MACHINE IS WITHDRAWN FROM SERVICE.

After that, nothing. Wondering what deviant microchip had caused this confessional crisis, I got up. The document was still in the printer. I took it and read: 'THe lady of THe CelestiAl RosE'. Underneath, the Cs and Ts and Hs had been regrouped into a repetitious and apparently meaningless series of word patterns:

HATE-TEACHER
CHEAT-HEART
HATE-HEART
CHEAT-TEACHER
HEART-CHEAT

Unable to make sense of this, I screwed the paper up into a ball, then thought better of it, smoothed it out, and put it in a back pocket. Then I set off down the steps.

There I paused to draw breath and consider what to do next. Obtaining a bike seemed my only hope. Perhaps the machine would be put back into service soon, and I could persuade it to accept an IOU for a bike. But when I turned round, the stairs and the room had vanished. I tried to retrace my steps, but couldn't find the stairway anywhere.

Then an idea occurred to me. It was so simple that I could not believe I had not thought of it before. If I walked back along the queue in the opposite direction, I would be bound to reach the entrance gates eventually. With renewed energy, I set off, walking against the flow of people.

By now I was feeling a little hungry and, as I was crossing a shopping plaza, I caught sight of a food shop. TERRY'S TASTEE TAKE AWAY SNAX, said the sign in peeling letters. Forgetting my lack of money, I went to investigate. The shop was boarded up.

I looked around me. The other shops were similarly abandoned, plateglass windows smashed or whitewashed, doors barred across with roughly nailed planks of wood. Rainwater puddles had collected inside the deserted shops and piles of discarded packaging, old newspapers, cigarette cartons and rusting cans had accumulated in the corners.

A rustling sound made me turn. Behind me a young boy was sitting in a pile of old hamburger cartons and cardboard boxes. He had in his hand a rusting tin with a faded orange label. Luckily I had my Souvenir of Babel Handy Pocket Knife with me, and offered to open the can for him, but before I had finished, he grabbed the tin from me and wolfed the contents in one gulp. I was rather annoyed at this and ticked him off sharply for his lack of manners. Then, forgetting he could not reply, I asked where I could find a café or food shop. He pointed upwards to where a huge banner hung across the square. In embroidered letters two foot high, it said:

THOSE THAT WILL NOT WORK SHALL NOT EAT
St Paul

I turned to question him further, but he had gone to sift through another pile of rubbish. So I set off again.

Walking in this direction, I could see faces instead of backs, and a strange thing now occurred to me. As I walked, I smiled hopefully, expecting an answering sign, a confirmation of my presence: a returned smile, a nod of the head. But none came. The crowds shuffled on their way, heads bowed, eyes lowered. The eyes that met mine were as blank as the concrete walls around them. I began to feel as if I did not exist. And then another strange sensation took hold of me. After some hours of walking and staring so hopefully into unknown faces, the faces began to seem familiar to me, as if I were seeing the same faces again for the second or third time. 'It's culture shock,' I told myself firmly. 'The strangeness of the place is beginning to affect you.'

To prove to myself that this was a delusion, I started to make a mental note of the faces in the queue: 'Young man, thirtyish, balding, denim jacket; old lady, blue rinse, flowery print dress . . .' After a time, rounding a corner, I saw not only 'young man, thirtyish, balding, denim jacket' and 'old lady, blue rinse, flowery dress', but also 'middle-aged family man, red sweatshirt, beerbelly' and 'young woman, blue skirt, red sandals, greasy hair'.

I stopped and leant against a parapet to absorb this new information. I had been going in circles. Below me the queue flowed and looped and intersected along the balconies and walkways. It was like the Labyrinth. If I had been equipped with foresight and a ball of string, perhaps I could have found my way out. But it was too late for the Theseus trick. Perhaps by noting down the room numbers I could at least keep a check on where I was going and avoid retracing my steps. I took notebook and pen out of my pocket and started off again.

But at that moment I caught sight of the old man who had spoken to me at the gateway. Overjoyed to see a familiar face, I ran up to him and seized his hands. 'I'm so glad to see you!' I cried. 'Please tell me how to get to the beginning of the queue.' But he seemed to have forgotten who I was. His eyes were glazed and expressionless. 'There is no beginning,' he said. 'The end then,' I said impatiently, 'the way out.' 'There is no end,' he said, 'and no way out.'

I looked at him. He had changed. His shoulders were bowed and he had adopted a shuffling gait. Now he looked just like everyone else in the queue. 'How did you get here?' I asked, in sudden curiosity. 'Were you rationalized?' 'No,' he said, 'I was retired here.' 'And what are you doing now?' I asked. As if reciting a litany, he replied, 'Possession of an owner-occupied dwelling negates Existence Sponsorship entitlement as do any liquid assets accruing from the sale thereof.' 'What do you mean?' I asked. 'Can you explain in my language?' 'When I stopped work,' he said, 'I had no money to live on. But they wouldn't give me any money because I owned a house. So I sold the house. But then they wouldn't give me any money because I had savings.' 'What happened then?' 'I spent my savings,' he said. 'They lasted three years.' 'So now they'll give you some money?'

For answer, he handed me the sheaf of forms. P3506 (pink) was headed: 'Application for Existence'. Underneath it said, 'Senior citizens desiring to apply for existence must complete forms Y023 and 504X before their application can be considered. Y023 (yellow) was headed: Declaration of Entitlement to Existence Sponsorship'. The declaration read:

> I wish to apply for Existence Sponsorship under the I AM GENEROUS scheme and hereby declare
> - that I am aged over 65, in possession of sound mind and body,
> - that I have no relatives living or other means of support,

- that the total funds in my possession amount to no more than 50 baubels,
- that I possess a valid existence permit.

Form 504X (green) was headed: 'Existence Permit'. Underneath it said:

> I wish to apply for an Existence Permit and hereby certify:
> a) my ability to provide no less than three months' rent in advance plus deposit of 500 baubels against damages,
> b) my entitlement to Existence Sponsorship.

There was one more form. 502B (grey) was entitled: 'Helpful Hints for Senior Citizens: a Government of Babel Document'. It read:

> We have done our best to streamline the process of validating existence and applying for sponsorship, but sometimes delay is unavoidable. These hints will help you cope in the intervening period.
>
> 1. As you get older, your appetite diminishes and you will find that your daily nutrition needs can be easily and simply satisfied with what you can find on the streets. You may even find you do not need to eat at all. However, for those who require it, a daily distribution of dinnerparty leftovers operates under the I AM GENEROUS scheme.
>
> 2. Although you will find that your food intake requirements have diminished, it is, nevertheless, wise not to think too much about food, or to frequent places where lavish meals are served. You will save yourself much unnecessary distress if you avoid these places.

3. As you get older, you will find that you have less energy than you used to have. To conserve energy and shoe leather, avoid walking too much. You may also find your need for sleep increasing. Many doorways have been conveniently provided for this purpose.

4. Newspapers are a good source of insulation in cold weather. Adequate supplies have been donated by the I AM GENEROUS scheme.

I handed the forms back to him. 'Where are you going now?' I asked. 'I haven't got the money for the Existence Permit, so I have to go to room 350H to collect form Y023.' 'You've already got Y023,' I said. He looked down at the forms in his hand. 'Why, so I have,' he said. His blank face registered no surprise. 'I'd better go now, or I'll lose my place in the queue.' I could not understand this. 'But why go? You've got the form.' He shrugged. 'It's the Process,' he said, as if that explained everything. 'It's the next step.' And he set off, shuffling into line behind the others.

I now had no idea what to do. This place was not a labyrinth, I realized: it was worse than a labyrinth. Labyrinths at least have beginnings and ends. This was more like a gigantic optical illusion, a mathematical figure like a Mobius strip, an endless eye-deceiving loop. As this realization slowly took root, another fact registered itself on my consciousness. The door opposite was labelled F408. It had a familiar ring. Then I remembered: the Aliens' Registration Room. It was a measure of how despondent I had become, that I now decided to go in.

The room was empty apart from the green glow of the computer screen. I sat down opposite the machine. 'Good afternoon, bonjour, buon giorno, guten Tag, buenos dias, namaste, ,' said the machine. 'Select greeting in appropriate language.' 'Good afternoon,' I typed. At once a question appeared on the screen. It was lengthy and complex, but quite direct.

'Can you produce evidence that your stay in Babel is temporary, that you have no relatives resident here, that you have no intention of marrying while you are here, that you will not attempt to find a job while you are here, and that you possess financial means of not less than 1000 baubels per week for the duration of your stay in Babel?' 'No,' I typed. Without hesitating, the screen replied, 'Undesirable Aliens are not welcome in Babel. Repatriation (at your own expense) will be arranged immediately. Type in personal details as they appear on your passport.'

I began, but had got no further than my name, when the machine interrupted. 'Please wait a moment,' it said, more politely than usual, and muttered to itself for a few minutes. Then an announcement appeared on the screen which took me completely by surprise. 'Your guide will be here in a few minutes,' it said. 'Would you like a cup of tea while you are waiting?' And to my amazement, it produced from somewhere deep within itself a china cup of sweet milky tea and a plate of biscuits.

It did not take me long to finish these, since it was now over eight hours since I had had breakfast. As I was slurping the last of my tea, a woman entered the room. It was Virgilia. It was not difficult to see that she was extremely angry. Despite this, I have never been so glad to see anyone, and told her so. With thin-lipped control, she asked, 'What have you been doing? What took you so long to get here?' I explained about my futile attempt to obtain a bike and to find the entrance. Her lips grew even tighter with suppressed anger and she said grimly, 'You must see that it's all your own fault for not following the Process. The machines are there to help you through difficulties. If you had done as you were told at once, you would have saved everyone a lot of worry and inconvenience. As it is, the rest of the group had to go on ahead, while I searched for you.' I apologized profusely, which mollified her somewhat, and she led me out onto the balcony outside.

'Where are we going?' I asked. 'To the Repatriation Room,' she replied. 'Now, since we're here, I suppose I'd better tell you something about the history and customs of the Basement, as you don't understand the lifestyle here and may have formed some mistaken impressions. Have you any questions?' I needed no encouragement. I was bursting with questions. 'What's everyone queuing for?' I asked. 'And what do people live on if they're not working? And what is Existence Sponsorship? And what is the I AM GENEROUS scheme?'

Virgilia seemed taken aback by all these questions. 'Goodness me, you have been busy!' she said. She sounded rather disapproving. But I must say she gave me a very patient and detailed explanation. 'The first thing you must understand,' she began, 'is that these people have deliberately chosen to come here. This poses a problem for the Babel government. We in Babel try to foster a society dedicated to the ideals of hard work, individual responsibility, self-reliance and enterprise. But we are also dedicated to the ideal of freedom: the individual's right to choose. The individuals here have chosen not to work. Now you could be moralistic and say that they are lazy. You could force them to work. But we in Babel do neither of those things. We firmly defend the individual's right to choose the lifestyle that suits him or her best, for choice is freedom, and the greater the availability of choice in a society, the greater freedom that society possesses.'

Although she was displeased with me, I must say it was wonderfully reassuring to be with Virgilia again. Things that had seemed confusing and disorientating before, now began to fall into place. 'So you allow them to live like this, although you disapprove of their lifestyle?' 'Exactly.' 'But what is all this queuing?'

Virgilia took a deep breath. 'Well,' she said, 'it's a kind of ritual, a folk custom that has survived into modern times and to understand that, we will have to go back in history. A long time ago, before the foundation of the Wealth Fair State, things had become so corrupt and degenerate that people were actually encouraged in this sybaritic lifestyle by the inducement of prizes donated by the Government. When you reached the end of the queue, you received a gift.' 'Like a treasure hunt?' 'Exactly. Well, you can imagine the consequences. No one saw the need for work, when living was so pleasant and comfortable without it. Babel became a land of lotus-eaters. The moral fabric of society had rotted through. We were bankrupt spiritually and financially. Well, of course, after the Liberation of the Ratepayers and the new ideology of Freed Man we stopped subsidizing indolence.' 'Do you mean that they still queue up, but there are no prizes?' 'Exactly. We realized that while we couldn't deny people the freedom to live as they chose, it was positively immoral to encourage their degeneracy with government subsidies. So we removed them. Not all at once, of course, that would have been too much of a shock. We made it more and more difficult to reach the end of the queue and little by little we decreased the value of the prizes until they ceased to exist.' 'But why do they still queue? What's the point?'

Virgilia sighed wearily and her tone became extremely patient. 'As I said, it's a kind of ritual. The form has survived without the meaning, as with all old folk customs. You don't think about the meaning of your actions when you throw confetti at a wedding, or say "Bless you" when someone sneezes, do you? Besides, it's good that they have something to occupy their time. Otherwise they would end up doing nothing at all.'

It was all beginning to make sense to me now. But something was still worrying me a little. 'But what do they live on, if they have no money? How do they exist? And why are all the shops closed?' 'We closed the shops some years ago, partly because the decline in purchasing power led to a decline in profits and the shops simply weren't paying their way. But also to combat the rising crime rate.' I looked puzzled and she explained, as if to a child, 'It's simply not fair to expose people to temptations they can't afford. Much better to remove the temptation altogether. We have had a much lower crime rate and much less social discontent since we banned the display of consumer goods in the Basement.'

'So what do people eat? How do they live?' 'Oh, that's where Existence Sponsorship and the I AM GENEROUS scheme come in.' 'I AM GENEROUS?' 'Individual Acts of Mercy and Generosity.' 'Oh, like charity?' 'Yes, a little. Although the Government feels it would not be morally justified in using public funds to support people in an unproductive and basically parasitic way of life, there are individuals who feel that they would like to help in some way, that their generosity might set an example to others and encourage them to mend their ways. There are two ways an individual can contribute: through the Scraps and Leftovers scheme, whereby kitchen leftovers are donated to the communal stewpot, or through Existence Sponsorship, which is a more personalized form of mercy, where the donor adopts an applicant and receives a photo and progress reports.'

Things were now falling into place and I began to see the logic behind things that had at first seemed so perplexing. I also realized how wrong we are to make instant judgements about another country without first trying to understand the culture and the history of that country and its people. It did seem to me that I had one or two more questions lurking at the back of my mind, but my attention was distracted by two incidents that occurred as we walked along the balcony that led to the Repatriation Room.

In front of us, in the queue, an old lady swayed, tottered and fell to the ground. Impassively, her fellow queuers stepped over her body and continued queuing. I started forward to help, but Virgilia restrained me. 'Don't worry,' she said, 'I expect she's having a little rest. Queuing can be quite tiring at her age.' As she spoke, two officials came up with a stretcher and loaded her onto it. 'Who are they?' I asked. 'Oh, they're from the Department of Harmony and Social Serenity. They are there to help with problems and ensure that things run smoothly,' explained Virgilia. 'I think she's dead,' I said, watching the officials carry away the body. 'Well, she was quite old,' said Virgilia soothingly. 'It's quite natural to die at her age. Turn right here, we're at the Repatriation Room.'

As we turned into the room, the second incident occurred. A crowd of men, women and children descended on me from all sides. Some held their hands out to me, some fell on their knees at my feet. One produced a filthy rag and began to rub my boots, one had a basket full of bunches of the wild yellow flowers I had seen growing on the wasteland and now pressed these into my hand. Some had drawn designs and pictures in chalk on the pavement, some, with upturned hats beside them, were playing flutes and whistles, while others fought to open the door for us. I was quite frightened at first, but they seemed to mean no harm and as we stumbled out of their clutches into the Repatriation Room, I asked Virgilia what it all meant. 'Another quaint local custom,' she replied, bolting the door firmly behind her. 'It's their way of saying goodbye to visitors.'

When I understood this, I found the custom quite charming, and wished I had accepted their tokens more graciously.

The Repatriation Room was filled with a great huddle of men, women and children, of all ages, shapes, sizes and colours from deepest black to palest coffee, all brightly dressed in their various national costumes. It was a picturesque and colourful sight. 'What are they doing here?' I asked. 'Waiting for a flight home,' replied Virgilia. She explained, 'Although people of other faiths and cultures are always welcome in Babel, sometimes when they arrive here they find the food does not agree with them, or they don't like the weather, or the local customs do not suit them. So we have a Repatriation Service for those who are feeling homesick.'

A second door led out of the Repatriation Room, and we made our way to this through the crowds, Virgilia nodding and smiling brightly to everyone we met, and stopping to ask them if they had enjoyed their stay in Babel and wishing them *bon voyage*. We went through the door and found ourselves on a moving corridor travelling swiftly between glossy white walls. The corridor led to the lift and we were able to catch an evening elevator to the Middle Floors and rejoin the rest of the group in the hotel, which is where, over a late-night glass of Scotch, I am writing this.

The Middle Floors

Babel, 22 May 1999

Yet another interesting day! I cannot stop marvelling at the endless variety of the human pageant and the innumerable forms of self-expression of the human spirit!

The day started with a rather strange breakfast of (you won't believe this!) raw oatmeal and a kind of solidified sour milk. Rick said it reminded him of the staple diet in Afghanistan or Tibet and Dorothy said she wouldn't say what it reminded her of. Most of my fellow travellers couldn't stomach it at all, but I am determined to try all the local foods here, so managed half a bowlful. Over breakfast the others told me about what they had done yesterday. On their way here they had had a most interesting excursion to the Second Floor (we're now on the third or fourth, I'm not quite sure – this whole area is called 'The Middle Floors'.)

What they had to tell me about working conditions there was quite amazing. I suppose my ideas are influenced by reading too many nineteenth-century novels! I would have expected to find clerks sitting on high stools, writing with quill pens in enormous ledgers, with a layer of dust and gloom over everything. Not so! Not a ledger or a pen in sight! And very few clerks. The whole place, apparently, was a forest of complicated equipment: TV screens, printers, telephones, copiers, computer terminals, calculators, satellite dishes, microphones, recorders, all connected by a tangle of wires, conveyor belts and leading to and from chutes appearing and disappearing out of nowhere.

What surprised them most, they said, was that wandering round among all this machinery, they met very few people. The local guide had explained that this area used to be overpopulated, but for the past decades the population had been decreasing, and was now at an acceptable level due to government measures such as Mirth Control. In the past, offices had been hopelessly overstaffed with such inessential functionaries as smiling clerks, error boys, deceptionists and tee-hee ladies, whose only role seemed to be to sit around drinking endless cups of tea, gossiping and cracking jokes. Under the Rationalization Drive, these had been phased out and since Total Automatization it had no longer been necessary to have people to carry out the office tasks. Machines could do them far more efficiently, quickly and cheaply. Since it was now only necessary to have a few workers on site to check and maintain the machines, the possibility of human error was almost nil.

A further improvement had been the elimination of the need to travel. In the old days, Second Floor inhabitants had had to travel vast distances to work on the Top Floor. Now, Top Floor bosses could simply issue instructions through the Intercommand, confident that the machines on the Second Floor would carry them out. The need for personnel displacement and interfloor contact was now obsolete; efficiency and productivity had increased; time-wasting and human error had been eliminated. All this had led to a dramatic reduction in the mirth rate.

I was rather sorry I had missed this interesting trip, even though I had had such a fascinating day myself. I was about to begin telling them about my experiences in the Basement, but at that point Virgilia interrupted, saying that it was time for the briefing for the morning's trip.

She began by telling us that we were going to be privileged to see a picturesque but nearly extinct way of life, a people who were fast being taken over by modernization but who clung stubbornly to their traditional way of life. These people and their customs were dying out, and in a generation or so would have ceased to exist, but for the moment continued in their unique and archaic lifestyle in their natural habitat, known as 'The Middle Floors', where they were one of the principal tourist attractions of Babel. It all sounded rather like Red Indian reservations in the United States.

At first sight the houses looked rather similar to the rows of little red-brick dwellings we had seen on the Ground Floor, but countless small details – panelled wooden doors, brass door knockers, dimpled or latticed window panes, carriage lamps, windowboxes, shutters, hanging baskets – gave the houses a quaint and old-fashioned air: more like country cottages than a town terrace. Miranda thought they were really sweet, but Klaus said that to the purist they represented a gross distortion of vernacular architecture. I thought it was all rather charming, and I found myself feeling nostalgic at the sight of these reminders of a bygone age and regretting that the wholesale modernization on the Ground Floor had led to the destruction of these original features.

Altogether I felt as if we had stepped fifty or a hundred years back in time, and this sensation was intensified when we turned a corner and came upon a colourful and busy market. Merchants were selling sacks of flour, oats, millet, sultanas, nuts, dried apricots, sesame seeds, lentils and beans of various kinds. Barrow-loads of vegetables: aubergines, peppers, courgettes, artichokes, asparagus, avocados, garlic. It was like going back to a world where convenience foods and interface shopping had never been heard of. A delicious smell of freshly baked bread wafted through the air: huge loaves of peasant bread were on sale in a baker's. Feeling hungry, I bought a roll, but found it heavy and indigestible, made with a kind of coarse brown flour.

Feeling thirsty, I went into another shop where the shelves were lined with rows of bottles containing juices and extracts of various fruits and vegetables, and selected one to try. The label said 'Extract of avocado, lime and dandelion', but as I opened it and raised it to my lips, the girl next to me burst out laughing and the assistant stopped me in horror. I couldn't understand much of what she said, as it was all very technical, but through an elaborate pantomime she made me understand that these fruit extracts were not for drinking, but for washing your hair! When I looked more closely at the labels on the pots and bottles of juniper, peach and marigold extract or elderberry and almond cream I found that the contents were described as 'Elbow rejuvenating lotion' or 'Ankle rub' or 'Moustache conditioner'. Ancient folk recipes, I suppose.

As I left the shop, something strange happened. The girl who had been behind me in the queue bent and picked something up from the floor. She looked at it and a startled expression came over her face. She made a movement towards me, then thought better of it and turned back towards the till and the assistant. The suspicion crossed my mind that I had dropped some money, which she had been about to give back, but had decided to keep. I almost returned to question her, but I had made such a fool of myself in the shop, that I could not face going back in. I consoled myself with the thought that the members of this peasant community probably needed the money more than I did and went on out into the street.

Next door, a herbalist hawked herb teas and various natural remedies, all promising immediate cures. Little shops sold brass door knockers, carriage lamps, windowboxes, hanging baskets, panelled doors, and shutters. Natives were everywhere, in their colourful costumes, busily chatting and bargaining. The women wore headscarves and flowered dresses and clogs with thick woollen stockings in bright colours: the men wore embroidered kaftans and tunics or coarse blue cotton trousers and thick homespun sweaters.

Everywhere shops sold native costumes: handwoven shawls, richly embroidered flowing skirts, handknitted garments in intricate designs. Stalls and pedlars sold handcrafted enamel jewellery or batik scarves dyed in natural fruit dyes. One shop sold crude, but not unattractive, peasant pottery: jars, mugs and pots in stone or earthenware; another sold handsewn patchwork silk cushion covers; yet another sold handcarved shoe-racks. I saw one shop selling nothing but handwoven teatowels, its neighbour was devoted exclusively to handpressed writing paper made from nettle leaves and elderflowers: 'an exquisite textural combination' said the sign, handwritten in beautiful copperplate. A sign over one shop advertised: HAND CHURNED CHEESE, while next door a woman laboriously turned a mill to produce wholemeal tagliatelli.

Automatization obviously did not exist here, and although I found the whole scene most picturesque, I began to pity the inhabitants for their hard and primitive lifestyle. (Though when I mentioned this to Virgilia, she sniffed. 'A touch of the marieantoinettes,' she said, dismissively. I asked her what a marieantoinette was, and she said a marieantoinette syndrome was a common psychological disorder affecting well-off people in comfortable homes who developed the delusion that they were eighteenth-century shepherdesses.)

But it was a wonderful place for souvenirs! We spent all morning there and I bought a pair of socks for Uncle Jim, handspun from Himalayan yak hair and knitted to a traditional herdsman's pattern; an attractive stoneware wine-cooler for Tim; a handwoven linen nightshirt trimmed with lace of a nineteenth-century Flemish design for Mavis; and a hand-turned sandalwood rattle for the baby. Miranda and I thought the market was the highlight of our visit here, but Rick said it was nothing compared to Marrakesh, and

Dorothy complained that you couldn't get a decent cup of tea anywhere. John the Baptist is in his element, however. He has bought a kaftan and some leather sandals and keeps saying that he thinks it's a really cool scene here. Hugo and Rosamund think it's all blissfully romantic. Tracey and Klaus are nowhere to be seen.

We had lunch in what Virgilia described as a typical restaurant on the 'village green'. Again I had the sensation that I had travelled back in time: the scrubbed wooden furniture, rush mats and crudely fashioned plates and dishes all made the place seem like a peasant's cottage of a century ago. But everything was quite clean, we were relieved to see, and, in fact, the place – though primitive – had a certain quaint rustic charm.

But the food was a different matter! If that's what they ate a hundred years ago, then I'm glad to be entering the twenty-first century! We began with what I can only describe as a 'mess of pottage': a murky brown substance, half liquid, half solid, which was described to us as 'lentil soup'. This was served with the coarse brown bread I had experimented with earlier. After the soup we had something called 'bean and parsnip moussaka with dandelion and nettle salad'. This was another brown substance, virtually indistinguishable from the first, though rather more solid and surrounded by a border of green leaves. We finished off with 'carrot and nasturtium syrup cake': an extremely solid brown substance, which left us feeling heavy and inert for the rest of the afternoon. To drink we could choose from nettle and elderflower wine, avocado juice or dandelion tea. I don't understand how they distinguish what they drink from what they write on, or rub on their ankles, or put on their hair. I suppose that must be one of the problems of living in an underdeveloped society – you have to maximize your use of the limited resources available to you.

In the centre of the table was a little earthenware pot of wild roses. They disturbed me slightly, though I couldn't make out why. They seemed to stir something in my memory. Suddenly I remembered. The mysterious message on the computer printout – wasn't there something about roses on that? I determined to ask Virgilia and tried to catch her attention while I fished in my pocket for the printout. But the piece of paper was no longer there. I began to wonder if I had imagined the whole thing; my experience in the Basement was beginning to seem more and more dreamlike. And when Virgilia finally turned to me with an impatient, 'Yes, what is it now?' I found myself at a loss for words. I stumbled and hesitated and did not know how to formulate the question. 'It doesn't matter,' I said at length, lamely. Virgilia raised her eyes to heaven, and turned to answer queries from Miranda who wanted to know where she could buy postcards of the adorable little houses, and Dorothy who wanted to know where she could find some Milk of Magnesia.

Lunch over, we all rose heavily from our seats and followed Virgilia out into the street. The afternoon programme was described as 'Visit to native dwelling, participation in craft workshop and other typical activities', so we plodded along in Virgilia's footsteps to a bright and pleasant little street, where red geraniums bloomed in the windowboxes, the door knockers were brightly polished and the dormer windows of the attic extensions gleamed in the afternoon sun.

Virgilia let us into one of the houses in the middle of the street. The interior was bare and spartan, but clean and bright – poor, but not degradingly so. The wooden floors were scrubbed and polished, and the simple pine furniture was spick and span. Here and there patchwork cushions, handloom rugs, posters and silkscreen wallhangings lent a splash of colour to the plain white walls and pine floors.

Logs crackled in the grate and in the wood-burning stove in the kitchen. A spinning wheel stood in one corner and the workshop extension was full of lathes and drills. Children's toys: wooden building bricks, vegetable-dye finger paints, and rag dolls in non-synthetic materials, were scattered over the floor in the playroom.

The house, like others we visited in the row, was deserted. 'Who lives here?' I asked Virgilia. 'Oh, teachers and social workers and other Public Surplus,' she replied, 'but right now they're probably all out at Hobby Hour.' 'Hobby Hour?' 'Yes,' she said. 'I'll take you there in a minute.'

Hobby Hour took place in a tastefully converted warehouse near the canal, where a placard announced: CREATIVE POTENTIAL FULFILMENT WORKSHOP. Virgilia handed us over to a local guide who gave us a brief introductory speech before taking us round. 'We on the Middle Floors,' he said, 'feel that time is best used in a productive and meaningful creative venture, so we felt the need to set aside a time each day where each individual could fulfil his or her own unique creative potential in the way that they personally felt was most experientially meaningful for them. In this way we can reach deep inside ourselves to the hidden wellsprings of creativity and self-expression that exist within every individual and affirm our unique human existence through self-realization. We must learn to discard our reliance on the ready-made products of the consumer society and to begin to explore our existence in new ways: to set off down the path of self-actualization through creative self-expression towards the goal of becoming fully actualized, many-faceted, totally realized human beings.'

Inside the warehouse, individuals were realizing themselves creatively in a multitude of different ways. Some of the women were plaiting rush baskets, making macramé roller blinds or carving mahogany desk tidies, while their menfolk made pottery candleholders or took classes in Afghan cookery.

I noticed that several of the women wore I AM GENEROUS badges and asked our guide what they had done to earn them. 'Probably contributed to the Existence Sponsorship scheme in some form,' he said. 'Let's ask Emma.' And he called one of the women away from her Interactive Massage Self-Help Group to explain to us. 'It's so wonderful,' she enthused. 'A few of us got together and formed an Action Committee. We put a few baubels aside every week and we have various fun-raising events like our Meditation for Action Rally or the Sponsored Self-Massage Evening and we send the proceeds into the Sponsorship Scheme. Then we get photos and reports and sometimes letters from the people we're helping. Even though we've never met them, I really feel they're part of the family in a way. It's so good to be *involved*. It's just so fulfilling to know that one's actions are *helping*, and to get the chance to *relate* in a caring way.'

Another woman came up to join us and Emma introduced us. 'This is Natasha,' she chirped. 'Natasha, show them the photos you got last week.' Natasha pulled a photograph from her hand-tooled leather shoulder bag. A grey-haired couple stared blankly out from the picture with rheumy eyes. Behind them was a peeling wall painted an institutional lime-green. 'Natasha's such a caring person,' said Emma, affectionately. 'She puts a bit aside every month to sponsor them, and she even sends them cards at Christmas. She never forgets. Not many people do that.' 'That's wonderful,' I said, staring at the wrinkled couple. 'And you don't even know them.' Natasha looked puzzled. 'Oh yes, I do,' she said, taking the photo and putting it back in her bag. 'They're my parents.'

It wasn't until a few minutes after this conversation, when we had passed through the Indonesian Tie-Dye Techniques workshop, the Aromatherapy for Beginners counselling session, the Naturists Against Acid Rain conference, Yoga for Toddlers, a How Transactional Analysis Can Enrich Your Family Life encounter group, an Inca Pottery Appreciation class, and a room where a seminar on 'Learning to Love Our Bodies' was taking place, that a question occurred to me.

'Why is everyone talking?' I asked Tristram, our guide. He seemed surprised. 'Meaningful communication is what the human experience is all about. Self-disclosure is necessary for personal growth and individual fulfilment. In our workshops here we try to create an atmosphere where individuals can self-disclose in a non-judgemental and non-threatening context. Self-awareness raising is part of the process of realizing our own unique growth potential. It's a step on the path to self-actualization and self-fulfilment, which is what the life-experience is all about.'

Because of the language barrier, our communication on this topic was not as meaningful as it might be, so I asked Virgilia when we met again, 'How is it that the people here can talk? I thought you said the speech function had been superseded.' 'Only on the Ground Floor,' explained Virgilia. 'Here, as you can see, people are rather behind the times. They still intermesh in a verbal dynamic.' 'Whereas the Ground Floor units interface more receptively?' I was beginning to catch on to the language. 'That's right,' said Virgilia. 'Talking is the Middle Floor lifemode. It's their reality-interface. They believe in relating.'

It was after this, as we left the building at the end of Hobby Hour, that I saw the girl. She was one of a group of people standing chatting on the warehouse steps before going back home. As we left the warehouse, I became aware that someone was staring at me. Her face looked oddly familiar, but when she caught my glance, she immediately looked away and resumed her conversation.

The incident preyed on my mind as Virgilia led us back to the hotel via a peep at a Pre-school Inner Exploration Through Waterplay group, but it was not until I had got back to my room and was changing into evening clothes for the Dinnerparty Tour that I realized who she was. The girl who was staring at me was the same girl who had laughed at me in the herbalist's shop. She must have taken my money: that would explain her embarrassment and the fact that she had pretended not to recognize me.

Much relieved, now that I had realized her identity and the reason for her odd behaviour, I went down to the hotel juice bar for a drink, which is where I'm now sitting, sipping a carrot and mango cocktail and waiting for everyone to assemble for this evening's excursion: the Dinnerparty Tour. More tomorrow, if I have time!

Babel, 23 May 1999

I'm writing this, with some difficulty, at the breakfast table. I have a splitting headache after last night's excursion – too much claret for me, I'm afraid! Oatmeal and sour milk are more than I can stomach this morning and so I'm drinking a cup of camomile and jojoba tea instead.

Last night's excursion was really most enjoyable. I haven't enjoyed myself so much since the Streetfight evening. We were well briefed on what to expect by Virgilia, who gave us each a leaflet called 'Dinnerparty Games' so that we would know the rules and be able to participate in the fun. There really were some very interesting and amusing games – and it wasn't too difficult to learn how to play. We must play some of them together when I get back. The names of the games were:

1. Character Assassination or Bugger Your Neighbour
2. Charades
3. Anecdote-capping or Anecdote Snap
4. Complaints Auction
5. Unhappy Families
6. Ladders
7. Outstrip Poker
8. Inter-course Intercourse

This tour took place in quite a different area of the Middle Floors, a couple of floors up. Here the houses were still made of red brick, but each was separated from the others: set apart in its own field of emerald green grass. High hedges and fences surrounded these fields, but it struck me as curious that I didn't see any sheep or other animals. I asked Virgilia where the farm animals were and she gave me a funny look and explained that the purpose of the fences was not to keep animals in but to keep people out. Apparently the square of grass has a symbolic significance for these town-dwellers as it reminds them of their country ancestors. They regard it as sacred ground and spend most of their spare time tending it carefully. No one is allowed to tread on it, as this would defile it, and all conversations must begin with a ritual observance on the state of the 'lawn' as it is called. And when I looked around me I could see, in the late evening sunlight, many householders carefully combing the grass into place, or blessing the earth by sprinkling it with holy water.

We were all assigned to different houses for the Dinner-party. Virgilia had prepared us for what would happen and explained how we should behave, so I knew what to expect. I knew for example that these people followed a cult of nature worship (because of their country origins) and that I should expect the house to be full of plants and vases of flowers or dried grasses, curtains and sofa covers to be made of flowered material, and pictures of flowers to be hanging everywhere. I knew too that I should begin by presenting an offering of a bouquet of flowers to the hostess and offer the host some complimentary remarks on the state of the lawn, and that I would not be allowed to see the children, who were considered unfit for human contact, but that I should be introduced to the dog, a holy animal held in some veneration by these people.

So I think I behaved correctly. I bowed low and laid my bouquet at my hostess's feet, while greeting my host, as I had been taught, with 'Lawn's looking lovely,' to which he replied, as I had been told he would, 'Could do with a drop of rain though.' I followed him through into the living room, casting my eyes down respectfully before the icons of pressed flowers in the hall. In the living room I wondered whether to genuflect before the family altar where vases of flowers stood on a shelf in front of a huge picture of sunflowers and over a hearth where a tasteful arrangement of bulrushes and pampas grass took the place of a fire, but decided instead to prostrate myself to the dog who came bounding to meet me. When my host had rescued me, saying apologetically, 'Bit frisky, I'm afraid. He's still just a puppy really,' drinks were served and a ring at the doorbell announced the arrival of the other guests.

As soon as the other guests arrived, everyone started playing Charades for all they were worth, and by the time we all sat down at table everyone was in a good mood for a round of Anecdote-capping. A game of Unhappy Families accompanied the hors-d'oeuvres and everyone went on to a Complaints Auction over the Grouse and Vintage Whines, with some frantic bidding for the titles of Highest Taxpayer and Victim of Local Council Stupidity. Over dessert the host had a private game of Ladders with his boss, while the rest of the table had a heated round of Outstrip Poker. The hostess and her best friend's husband volunteered to do the washing-up after dessert, while the rest of us had a rousing session of Bugger Your Neighbour. They reappeared after what seemed a very long time with the coffee and After Hate Mints, and the evening was over. The only game we didn't seem to play was Inter-course Intercourse. I was rather disappointed by this, as I had been looking forward to it, but Dorothy, who was allocated to the house next door, said that they played it all evening and it was really boring.

The others are beginning to struggle down to breakfast now, clutching their heads and groaning, so I'll stop writing. Virgilia says we are to visit some educational establishments today. More later!

Babel, 23 May, morning

John the Baptist has gone native! He has joined some Encounter Group Commune or Commune Encounter Group and told Virgilia that he thought he'd pass on the Top Floor experience and hang loose here for a while. The rest of us assembled after breakfast and made our way through streets full of early-morning joggers and mothers taking their children to Pre-school Play Experiences or Socialization Events. On the way a thought struck me. It seemed to me that I had not seen any educational establishments on the Ground Floor. And surely the children in the Basement queues should have been at school. (For some reason it did not occur to me to wonder about education in the Streetlife sector.)

I voiced my query to Virgilia, who, as usual, had an answer. 'The Education mode was found to be a non-viable interrelationship below Floor Three,' she said. 'We did an efficiency-cost-effectiveness survey and found that the productive time-utilization factor was approaching zero. The trouble was that the linguistic modes did not intermesh and teachers and pupils became locked in a negatively confrontational behavioural mode. 'Negatively confrontational?' 'Too many teachers were getting killed,' she said. 'This offered, of course, a potential solution to the overstaffing problem, but the public outrage factor was a little too high.' 'So you put a stop to Lower Floor education?' Certainly not,' said Virgilia huffily. 'How many times do I have to tell you that the Babel government never "puts a stop" to anything. We are the party of individual choice and freewill. We believe that the individual must act as his or her conscience advises, not as the State dictates.' 'So what happened?' 'We increased the personal choice factor in education and the problem solved itself.' 'Do you mean that you let the children choose whether to go to school or stay at home?' 'No, no, no,' said Virgilia impatiently, 'that's progressive education. That's another thing entirely. We let the parents choose which school to send their children to and we allowed the schools to be responsible for their own finances. Increasing individual choice and encouraging initiative.' 'So what happened?' 'Well, obviously,' she said, 'no one opted for the schools with counterproductive learning modes. These then became economically unviable.' 'So?' 'So they had to close down of course,' she said. 'Survival of the Fattest. The first law of economic efficiency.' 'But didn't the other schools become overcrowded?' I asked. She looked at me pityingly. 'Just think about it for a minute,' she said. 'If they had opened their doors to anyone and everyone, then no one would have wanted their children there either. It would have been economic suicide.' 'So what happened?' Virgilia was growing tired of this conversation. 'As I told you,' she said, 'the problem solved itself. Besides, what would those children do at school? They can't read or write, they can't speak. They can't even understand the language.'

We had now reached the school, a collection of grim red-brick buildings with high windows. Outside, on the asphalted playground, groups of children were chasing around, playing Skins and Pakis or Stockbrokers and Taxmen. I caught the words of an old counting rhyme sung by a group of children:

Eeny meeny miny mo
Catch a Yuppie by the toe
If he sells out let him go
Eeny meeny miny mo.

Nearby, girls were skipping to the chant:

John buys coffee
John sells tea
John has shares in
GEC.

John buys low
John sells high
John has bought up
ICI.

or

On the carphone there's a lady
Who she is I do not know
All she wants is gold and silver
All she wants is a tax-free sum
So call in her stockbroker
Stockbroker, stockbroker

So call in her stockbroker
And open the champagne.

A whistle blew and the children raced for the entrance of the school, pushing, shoving and kicking in an effort to get there first. I was touched by their enthusiasm for learning. We picked our way through the debris of torn blazers, crumpled caps, scuffed shoes and trampled bodies left behind by the scrum and made our way to a classroom.

A lively scene met our eyes. Paper aeroplanes and desklids whizzed through the air. The air was filled with the enthusiastic yells of the students, punctuated by the occasional tinkle of breaking glass as a beer can or whisky bottle flew through a window. A small group sat in one corner quietly folding paper aeroplanes, while near them another group were preparing miniature warheads. Most of the class, however, were encamped behind two barricades of upturned desks, from which vantage points they hurled insults and petrol bombs at each other.

In my day, classrooms used to be rather dull places. I had heard a lot about the benefits of group work but had never expected to find it so enthusiastically received. This particular classroom was so learner-centred that it took me some time to find the teacher, who was crouching down on his hands and knees behind the desk at the front of the room. I joined him there and, as the missiles flew over our heads, he explained to me that the new syllabus was project-centred, theme-based and focused on experiential learning and that this was a Practical Empathy Hour. As the bell rang, I asked him what subject he was teaching. 'Peace Studies,' he replied, ducking a paper aeroplane with gelignite warhead and preparing for a dash to the door.

I followed him into the corridor, where my attention was

caught by peals of innocent childish laughter coming from a classroom across the way. I entered it and found a creative writing class in full swing. Children armed with aerosols of brightly coloured paint were decorating the peeling lime-green walls from top to bottom with original and inventive slogans. The pride and delight they took in their own work was evident. The works that earned the roars of appreciation that I had heard were SIR IS A WANKER! and SIR FUKS GERBILS! I asked Sir why he did not correct the spelling in the last poem and he told me disapprovingly that it could be very harmful to a child's creative development to impede the flow of uninhibited self-expression; indeed it could lead to all sorts of traumas and hang-ups in later life. He made me feel rather guilty for having asked the question and I wondered uneasily what character defects I owed to my own rigid education.

I spent a very interesting morning in the school and peered into several classrooms where lively and fascinating lessons were going on. I sat in on a science class where white-coated pupils were enthusiastically preparing and inhaling a whitish powder, and a biology class where small groups were doing creative and inventive practical work on the Human Body amid piles of discarded blazers, shirts, trousers and navy-blue knickers. Last of all I visited a most enjoyable cookery class where pupils were preparing a barbecue over a bonfire of chairlegs and desklids. I wanted to ask what they were cooking, but the teacher responsible was nowhere to be found.

As I walked around I became conscious that I was feeling a little puzzled about something, and as the time came to leave I realized what it was. During the whole morning in the school I had not seen a single book. I asked Virgilia why. 'Oh, the book is a long-outmoded educational concept,' she explained. 'Firstly, books are not really cost-effective. The where?-and-tear factor is just too high and simply doesn't justify initial outlay. And secondly, it was realized some time ago that education is about skills, not about content. So why do you need books? You can't get experience from a book.'

As we left the school and began to descend the steps, we were swept backwards and almost crushed by a veritable army of stout women in helmets and riotshields who stormed up the stairs in battle formation. Picking myself up and dusting myself down, I said to Virgilia, 'Who were they?' 'Dinner ladies,' she replied, retrieving her shoes and casting around for the buttons from her blouse.

When we had stuck the heels back on her sandals and safety-pinned her blouse together, we set off back to the hotel and I began to express my appreciation of what I had seen during the morning. Virgilia cut me short. 'Idiotic liberal idealists!' she snorted. 'See the mess they make of everything!' I was surprised. I had thought we were visiting a model school. But Virgilia made me understand that since the Middle Floors were something of an anachronism, educational theory there was also stuck in a time-warp. The teachers there thought that they were doing their best to bring out and develop certain innate human qualities such as creativity, compassion, tolerance. 'But happily the children know better,' said Virgilia. 'They've got enough sense to reject all this wishy-washy idealism. They look to the future not the past. Where would tolerance get you in today's world? What we should be instilling in children is the spirit of competition. Initiative. Drive. A bit of aggression. Greed.' 'So what will happen to the children?' I asked. 'Well,' said Virgilia, 'as I told you, this is a rapidly disappearing culture. The children are rejecting their parents' values. And rightly so. What has all this creativity done for their parents?' 'So will they leave?' I asked. 'Where will they go?' 'If they have enough initiative, probably either to Streetlife or the Stockmarket,' said Virgilia. 'The entry qualifications are roughly the same.'

Before I finish this letter, I must confess to something. I have the strange sensation that I am being followed. On our way back to the hotel after the Dinnerparty Tour last night, I thought I heard footsteps following us down the street, but when I turned and looked there was no one there. I put the experience down to too much claret at dinner, but the same thing happened this morning on our way back to the hotel from the school. This time I retraced my steps to the last corner and looked back down the street, just in time to catch a glimpse of an embroidered red skirt disappearing into a doorway.

Babel, 23 May, teatime

An odd incident occurred during our trip this afternoon, which goes some way to solving the Mystery of the Red Skirt, but which has left me even more puzzled than I was before. But first things first. Let me tell you about our visit to the university campus.

Our morning's experience at the school led to a lively exchange of views over lunch. Miranda said the little kids were just darling and Hugo and Rosamund thought that the atmosphere in the school was delightful and that the teachers were doing a wonderful job in fostering a climate of imaginative involvement and creative self-expression, but Dorothy thought the row was terrible, it got on her nerves, she couldn't be having to do with all that noise and in her opinion what those kids needed was a good hiding and being made to sit down and learn their three times table. Klaus offered us all an illuminating analysis of Babel educational history, the Italian made a few jottings in his book and Tracey and Rick were not available for comment.

Virgilia reiterated the principles of Babel educational philosophy: that a school was, like anything else, a consumer product, and that it was up to the parents to select a school according to their personal taste and the means available to them – in this case the school was a reflection of Middle Floor culture and Middle Floor finances. Like everything else, schools were subject to market forces and the laws of supply and demand: if the educational principles and financial arrangements on which they were based were not sound, then they would go into liquidation.

By now I had several questions for Virgilia, and she, judging by the weary expression on her face, was expecting them. 'You said this was an old-fashioned school. What are the other kinds of school like? What are Top Floor schools like? And how are schools financed? Who pays?' Virgilia sighed deeply and began to explain. 'I don't know if you'll have time to visit a Top Floor school, but they are generally considered excellent. Of course the principles and financial backing behind them are much sounder. It is possible for parents to choose from various types of school, of course, according to choice-personalization and value-differentiation, whether they want their children to specialize in Management or Finance, for example. But in general most parents want their children to go to a school where they will Learn The Rules and Play The Game. As for finance, schools used to be financed by the State, but this was a very unsatisfactory arrangement.' 'Why?' 'Mainly because there was no money available.'

'So what happens now?' 'Well, the parents contribute money for the upkeep of the buildings and pay into a fund for teachers' salaries, and will sometimes have a little fund-raising effort for special causes like a new swimming pool, or a teacher's retirement pay. We found that people appreciate things so much more if they feel they are contributing something of themselves. But the schools are also subsidized.' 'By the Government?' 'No, by businesses.' 'How does that work?' 'Well, firms may make generous donations for image-enhancement purposes: for example, the Silver Leaf Tobacco Company recently donated several sports centres to schools, Matthews Chocolates have financed several oral hygiene departments, while Pornojunk Films often make gifts of video facilities. But, basically, all the courses offered at schools are sponsored by businesses: banks may finance accounting courses, or software firms may set up computer labs. It all depends on the firm's needs and how many new trainees it requires in specific areas.'

'Do you mean that firms determine the curriculum?' 'Of course. What other possible practical way is there of financing schools, of tying what is taught in schools to market forces, of regulating supply and demand? Otherwise you would get an absurd situation where there was a surplus of children studying nuclear physics, for example, and not enough studying investment management. Worse still, you could get a situation where thousands of children were learning completely unnecessary subjects, such as history or literature. You won't believe it when I tell you, but this actually was the case ten years ago or so. Incredible, isn't it?'

But I had drifted off the immediate subject during this lengthy explanation, and my mind had been toying with another question, which I now put to Virgilia. 'You said that the Middle Floor kids were rejecting their parents' values and would probably end up emigrating. Does this mean that you're allowed to travel freely from one module to another?' 'Yes, of course,' said Virgilia. 'Where do you think you are? Outer Mongolia? Need I remind you that we in Babel have a society founded on the highest of all human ideals: freedom and . . .' But I was still pursuing my own line of thought and rather rudely interrupted her: 'So anyone can live anywhere they choose?' 'Naturally,' said Virgilia. 'You just have to be able to speak the right language. And have the right financial basis,' she added as an afterthought. I was intrigued. 'So, if you speak a different language you can go to a different module?' 'Of course,' said Virgilia, 'that's the basis of the Sealed Concept Group policy.' 'And are these languages taught in school?' 'Of course not,' said Virgilia. 'Languages aren't necessary, unless you want to be an Inlinguist guide. In any case it would be contrary to the Minimize Discord policy.' 'So how do people learn new languages?' 'Well,' said Virgilia, 'haven't you noticed that children very rarely grow up to speak the same language as their parents? And, especially around adolescence, a youngster's language will begin to diverge from the norm of the module, or he will begin to formulate non-norm-centred concepts. The mid-thirties or round about forty is another period carrying a high risk of language crisis potentiality.' 'So what happens then?' 'Well,' she replied, 'in the case of norm-centred linguistic deviance, specially trained staff will help deviants over their language crisis and facilitate adaptation to a different language mode, and after a short linguistic rehabilitation period they will be transferred to the appropriate module.'

'Is there such a thing as a non-norm-centred linguistic deviant?' I asked. 'And what does it mean?' 'Someone who speaks a language that doesn't correspond to any of the languages spoken in any of the modules.' 'Are there any non-norm-centred deviants?' 'Certainly. It's rare, but it occurs.' 'What do you do with them?' For once she didn't quibble about my use of words. 'We transfer them to the University,' she replied. 'But then no one would understand them?' 'Exactly,' she said and went on, 'sometimes it even occurs that a unit will begin quite spontaneously to speak a language that has never existed before.' 'What do you do then?' I asked. 'Oh, it's very simple,' she said. 'We transfer them to Religions. We're scheduled to go there tomorrow.'

After lunch we drove to the University, an assembly of glass and concrete structures in rectangular or rhomboid shapes. The buildings were surrounded by lily ponds and were linked by small arching bridges or by stepping stones moulded out of concrete in fanciful shapes. Around the perimeter stood a ramshackle collection of Nissen huts and Portacabins. Virgilia had arranged for a boat tour of the campus, and I found myself, together with Hugo, Rosamund and Dorothy, in a small wooden boat rowed by the Professor of Anthropology. 'It's awfully good of you,' said Dorothy politely, 'to take time off from your students to row us round the campus.' 'Students?' he queried. I remembered Virgilia's words about non-norm-centred deviants and for an awful moment thought that we wouldn't be able to communicate at all. But then he explained, 'Oh, that's all right, they're both having a tutorial with my colleague at the moment. Besides,' he added, 'we have to make money somehow.'

Any hopes of successful communication roused by this utterance were, however, dispelled, when he began the running commentary on the campus scenery. Wheezing and puffing as he pulled on the oars, he began, 'In this campus you see a skilful use of architecture as myth, architecture as significant of a primary opposition (I am of course talking about the nature–culture paradigm, the relationship between the raw and the cooked as it were) symbolized in the aquatic and the terrestrial. In this case, where the signifier is water, the signified is nature, the raw; concrete, on the other hand, is signific-ant of culture, the cooked, though perhaps if one is referring to some departments in this university 'half-baked' might be a better adjective.' He wheezed and puffed so heartily at his own joke that he caught a crab and nearly lost an oar.

Recovering his balance, he went on, 'Another significant matrix is encoded in the fluid–concrete paradigm: the opposition between fluidity and what one might venture to call concretality, if I may coin a phrase. So we have the fluid: the unknown, the unformed, the uncharted, the as-yet-uncodified; and the concrete: the known, the formed, the charted, that which is encoded. But here we run into a paradox, a difference, or perhaps, we might say, *differance*. For the concrete is also a container and that which is within a container (I mean, of course, the contained) is fluid; the young minds which are here to be formed are also fluid, uncharted, unencoded. One might even take this a little further: it is perhaps not altogether fanciful to suggest that the nature of knowledge itself is not concrete but fluid, eternally changing, taking the shape of the vessel in which it is contained. So we must ask ourselves the question: which is *a priori*: knowledge or the form in which it is known to us? What we know or how we express it? *Langue* or *parole*? Which came first: the signified or the signifier?'

He paused and leant on his oars, lost in thought. I looked at my travelling companions. Dorothy had dropped off to sleep. Hugo and Rosamund had obviously found both signified and signifier in each other's eyes. Embarrassed, I looked over to where one or two of the contained had escaped their container and were sitting thoughtfully at the water's edge, reading, smoking and dabbling their feet in the water. A charming idyll of academic life, I thought, though as we drifted closer it became apparent that what was significant for them was encoded in the pages of *Macho!* magazine.

The silence was broken by the Professor, who resumed abruptly, 'But so far we have said nothing of the syntagmatic relationship!' Dorothy woke up with a start and, pretending she had been awake all along, said 'Oh, my goodness, how could we have forgotten that?' The Professor continued, 'Think of the bridges, think of the stepping stones!' 'It cannot have escaped your notice,' he went on, 'that all the blocks, all the buildings, all the complexes, all the what we might call "facult-emes", are interconnected. Thus Physics is connected with Mathematics and Music with Geology. Even Philosophy is connected to the rest of the University, however perilous the stepping stones may seem!' And again he succumbed to an attack of gasping and wheezing.

Waving one oar in demonstration of his point, he continued, 'Thus one may see metaphorically, or perhaps metonymically, signified, the interconnectedness, one might say, the holism of knowledge. Though if we are to look at it another way (and indeed our duty is to look at it another way) to deconstruct, as it were, the perspective we have just established, one might say the significance (or perhaps even the *signific-ence*) lies in the Gap rather than in the Bridge. For there can be no doubt that the Gap is *a priori* to the Bridge, that in a sentence the spaces between the words, as it were, are as important as, and perhaps even in a sense define the words themselves. And thus it is with . . .'

He was interrupted by an exclamation of disgust from Rosamund who had been trailing her hand dreamily in the water. Among the blossoming lilypads she had encountered several cigarette butts and a used condom. 'Ah yes,' said the Professor thoughtfully. 'The fresh and the decayed. The growing and the spent. Fertility and anti-fertility . . .' We had drifted into the mud. Fortunately it was not too far to the Geology Pier, and it was there that we bade goodbye to our dripping and mud-stained guide. We thanked him for his kindness. 'Well,' he said, shaking our hands, 'I do hope I have been able to demystify things a little for you.'

There were still a few things, however, that continued to mystify me, and as we negotiated the stepping stones to the Science Faculty, I made a mental note of questions to ask Virgilia, who would be waiting for us at the Levi-Strauss Memorial Landing Stage. But as we crossed a windswept expanse of concrete, a white-coated figure scurried down the steps of the Medical and Biological Sciences building. He was clutching a tin, which he proffered on reaching us, panting, 'Care to make a donation to the work of the department?'

I reached in my pocket for my loose change. Hugo and Rosamund followed suit, but Dorothy enquired cautiously, 'What exactly *is* the work of your department?' 'Cancer research,' he replied, watching as we dropped the baubels into the collecting tin. 'I can't thank you enough for this generous contribution,' he went on. 'I hate to have to trouble you like this, but funds are a little short at the moment. The department shop's not doing too well, the Spring Fayre was rained off and sales of our Herbal Tonic Wine and Test Your Own Urine Kit have dropped quite dramatically recently.'

I tried to understand the implications of this. 'But doesn't your department get funded?' I asked. He paused on his way up the steps and turned to look at me. 'I was forgetting you were tourists and don't understand the system,' he said. 'But just think about it for a moment. Who would fund us? Tobacco companies? Aerosol manufacturers? Fast food producers? Whisky distilleries? Even pharmaceutical companies are worried we might discover some side-effects.' 'And don't you get any money from the Government?' I asked. He shook his head thoughtfully, remembering. 'A long time ago we used to get what were known as government grants. But in one of the Rationalization Drives it was decided that it just wasn't cost-effective any more to keep people alive. So now we have to finance ourselves. Would you care to come in and see the department?' he added. Dorothy thought she had had enough Education for one day, and her bad leg was playing up, so she went on to the landing stage; but Hugo, Rosamund and I followed the Professor up into the Medical Research Department.

I was surprised by the lively atmosphere. The place was a hive of activity. The corridor walls were plastered with posters advertising a variety of events from three-day intensive acupuncture courses (350 baubels) to faith healing evenings (75 baubels) and the whole of the ground floor was taken up with a supermarket where you could buy decorative pill bottles, toy X-ray machines, skeleton dolls and souvenir tea towels emblazoned with a diagram of the respiratory system. On the second floor was a Health Foods café, where we each had a glass of the Professor's Tonic Herb Wine, and the top floor had been made into a kind of amusement arcade, where you could get a souvenir X-ray portrait (15 baubels), throw acupuncture needles at a cardboard cut-out of the human body (10 baubels with 20 baubels prize if you hit the right pressure points), guess how many pills were in the bottle (5 baubels a go), have a special massage from Physio Fanny (adults only, 60 baubels), watch a video of an operation (10 baubels), test your own blood pressure (15 baubels with 30 baubels prize if you could make the gauge hit 150) or enter a raffle for a home ECG machine.

A couple of things still puzzled me though, and while Hugo and Rosamund were seeing how far they could make each other's blood pressure rise, I asked the Professor where he taught the students and did his research. 'Ah, students,' he said vaguely, rather as the anthropologist had done, 'we don't seem to be getting many students these days. And as for my research, we had to move my lab to make way for the amusement arcade.' 'Where is it now?' I asked. He pointed out of the window to one of the Portacabins on the far side of the lily pond. 'Not that I get much time to go there now,' he said. 'Running the Enterprise Zone has become more-or-less a full-time job.' Perhaps it was my imagination, but I thought he sounded a little wistful.

I had thought Virgilia would be annoyed by our late arrival, but in fact we were not the last. She was still waiting for one of the other groups, who had been diverted into trying the Oceanography Department's Underwater World (Skin Diving and Snorkelling Amid Fantastic Coral Gardens, 30 baubels a time, snorkel and flippers extra). While we were waiting, I asked her why there were so few students, and if the other universities were similar. 'Other universities?' she queried, 'This is the only one left.' 'What happened to the others?' 'They just weren't economically viable. They couldn't make ends meet and so they went bankrupt. The trouble is that a lot of these academics have absolutely no business sense. You have to balance the books if you're running a business, you know. And then there just isn't the demand for their product any more.' 'Do you mean that no one wants to study?' 'Why on earth should they?' she said, reasonably. 'Who in their right mind would want to spend three of the best years of their life cooped up in a dry-as-dust university studying some irrelevant subject when they could be playing their part in the vital job of wealth creation? Ensuring a future for their family? Doing their bit to make Babel great? No,' she sighed, 'thankfully young people these days have become too aware of their social responsibilities to waste their time in such self-indulgent . . .' She was in fine flow, but was interrupted at this point by the arrival of the snorkellers, clutching souvenir trophies of coral and conch shells, and the subject of the relationship between education, economics and social responsibility was dropped as we all set off back to the hotel.

It was then that the incident occurred. As we left the university gates, a girl on a bicycle swerved erratically and collided with me. Neither of us was hurt, but as I picked myself up I realized something with a shock. It was the girl again! The one who had laughed at me in the herbalist's shop, the one who had stared at me so intently on the warehouse steps, the one who, I realized as I saw her embroidered red skirt, had followed me down the street. I opened my mouth to ask her who she was and why she was pursuing me, but she had already mounted her bike. Mumbling an apology, she pushed off past me, at the same time pressing something into my hand. It was a small crumpled piece of paper. At first I thought she had repented of her action and was returning the money to me, but when I opened my hand and looked at it I found not a banknote but a small piece of white paper. I turned to try to catch her by the arm, but she had pedalled off into the distance.

I have the piece of paper in front of me now. It is the computer printout I thought I had lost. An unknown hand – the girl's? – has doodled on the paper, drawing loops and circles around the letters, and at the bottom, clumsily printed, are the words: MEET ME HERE AT SIX.

Babel, 23 May, midnight

In the end it was not too difficult to slip out of the hotel unnoticed. The others were all exhausted from the day's sightseeing and had retired to their rooms while Virgilia had gone to see to the documentation for the next stage of our journey. I thought it best not to tell anyone where I was going, although I was mystified by this apparent need for secrecy. Why didn't the girl come and meet me here? Why didn't she speak to me, instead of following me down the street and passing me cryptic notes? So it was with a mixture of feelings that I left the hotel: excitement, curiosity, bewilderment – but also a strange resentment whose source I didn't properly understand. I was tired. I wanted to relax and enjoy my holiday. I was annoyed with the girl for arranging the meeting in this unorthodox way.

When I got to the gate there was no one around. Then a figure materialized from the twilight, pushing a bike. It was unmistakably the girl, her red skirt flapping round her calves as she strode authoritatively through the shadows. I moved forward to join her. 'Follow me,' she said. 'And carry these. Then you'll look like a student.' And she thrust a great pile of papers into my arms. I opened my mouth to question her, but she was already striding on ahead of me. Meekly I followed her to the bike shed, then across a line of stepping stones to a low concrete building and up a dingy flight of stairs to a room on the first floor. She snapped on the light and I put down my pile of papers with a sigh of relief.

'Thank you for delivering the message,' she said. 'Message?' I had no idea what she meant. 'The message about the Charter,' she said, as if it were self-evident. 'Charter?' 'Oh, perhaps you didn't realize it was about the Charter. After all it was in code.' 'Code?' I was beginning to feel like an echo chamber. 'Yes, look at the paper,' she said. I took the paper from my pocket. 'It's all there,' and she pointed to the loops and doodles around the words the machine had so frantically printed. I stared at the paper.

'The capital letters in the first line spell CHARTER,' she said. 'No they don't,' I objected. 'Well, almost, and anyway it's repeated again and again in the rest of the message.' I stared at the encircled letters:

HATE-TEACHER
CHEAT-HEART
HATE-HEART
CHEAT-TEACHER
HEART-CHEAT

It still didn't make sense to me. 'I think you're making a mistake,' I began. 'I know nothing about this. What happened was . . .' She broke into my explanation. 'It doesn't really matter how it happened. What is important is that we got the message. Now, if you agree to deliver the Charter for us . . .' She broke off. Her eyes moved to the door and she appeared to be listening. I could hear the sound of footsteps, of many footsteps, coming down the corridor. She looked around her. 'Quick, in here.' She snapped off the light and pushed me in through what seemed to be a cupboard door. I looked around in the dim half-light. It had obviously been some kind of book store, for the walls were lined with bookshelves, all now empty and festooned with cobwebs. 'Now look here,' I began. 'What on earth is happening?' She put a hand over my mouth. 'Quiet,' she hissed. 'It's Incpol.' 'Inkpoll?' I echoed stupidly. 'Incpol. The Income Police. They're here to make the Cuts.' 'What cuts?' She laid her finger to her lips and we stood there in silence while the sound of footsteps grew louder and louder, then passed the door and receded into the distance. Somewhere down the corridor a door slammed. The footsteps clattered down a flight of stairs. Outside, a car engine revved up and roared away. Then silence. I looked at the girl. She had visibly relaxed but her eyes were still watchful. She spoke rapidly, still in a whisper. 'Look, I'd better go now. If you meet me here at the same time tomorrow I'll be able to give you the Charter.' I opened my mouth to . . . to what I don't know. To protest, to ask what she meant, but she was already at the door, looking right and left down the corridor, then with a quick backward glance and a nod to me over her shoulder, she had gone.

I walked slowly back to the hotel, my mind buzzing with questions. Who was she? What was this mysterious charter? Who were Incpol? What was the connection between her and the machine in the Basement? What did she want me to do for her? Above all, did I want to get involved? I felt torn between curiosity and a reluctance to get embroiled in what seemed to be such a mysterious and complicated affair. Wouldn't it be more sensible to forget the whole crazy episode and get on with enjoying the tour? God knows I need the holiday. Even as I asked myself the question, I knew the answer. My curiosity would get the better of me. Of course I would go tomorrow.

Babel, 24 May 1999

I went to bed last night with my mind full of the day's events and drifted off eventually into a confused sleep, where at one moment footsteps pursued me down endless echoing corridors and at another I was crawling through a jumble of giant letters heaped crazily on top of each other.

At breakfast I was feeling disturbed and grumpy, and I am afraid I was rather short with Dorothy who wanted to tell me about her gallstones and show me pictures of her grandchildren. My mood lasted all morning, which was left free for last-minute souvenir shopping, but all thoughts of yesterday's intrigue were driven from my mind by our afternoon trip to the high security module known as Religions, Cults and Alternative Lifestyles.

Imagine a huge temple with a multitude of roofs of all sizes and shapes: steeples and towers, of brick, of stone, of slate, bare and ivy-clad, spires twisted like barley sugar, bulbous onion domes and golden cupolas, curving green-tiled roofs, gilded pagodas, pinnacles and turrets outlined against the skyline. That's what we saw as the security guard swung back the heavy carved wooden doors leading to Religions, Cults and Alternative Lifestyles. I had never seen anything like it and Miranda's round brown eyes nearly popped out of her head with amazement, but Rick said it was nothing like the temples in Khajuraho, and Klaus said that to his mind the mélange of cultural modes was aesthetically unappealing.

We approached the temple via a courtyard and a flight of marble steps. Stone figurines of saints and gurus stood in the courtyard next to gilded and jewelled statues of demons and dragons and political leaders; gargoyles and devil's masks grinned down at us from the eaves. Inside the temple was a vaulted entrance hall with a large and many-armed signpost. METHODISTS, said one arm; CATHOLICS, said another. Other signposts read: COPTS, JEWS, SPIRITUALISTS AND UFO OBSERVERS, CND ACTIVISTS AND PEACE PROTESTERS (INCLUDING QUAKERS), HINDUS, MUSLIMS (SHI'ITE), MUSLIMS (SUNNI), ENVIRONMENTALISTS, VEGETARIANS (NON-BUDDHIST), VEGANS (NON-JAIN), ANIMAL RIGHTS ACTIVISTS, RADIO HAMS, ENCOUNTER GROUPS, FAITH HEALERS, HARE KRISHNA, FUNDAMENTALISTS, BUDDHISTS (THERAVADA), STRUCTURALISTS, POST-STRUCTURALISTS, QUANTUM PHYSICISTS, ASTROLOGERS, BAPTISTS, CHILDREN OF GOD,

SATANISTS, SOCIOLOGISTS, PSYCHOTHERAPISTS, LEFTISTS, FAR LEFTISTS, MARATHON RUNNERS, FEMINISTS, BUDDHISTS (ZEN), THEOSOPHISTS, DOOMSDAY WATCHERS (APART FROM NUCLEAR DISARMERS AND ENVIRONMENTALISTS), SOCIAL DEMOCRATS, LIBERAL DEMOCRATS, LIBERAL AND SOCIAL DEMOCRATS, BUDDHISTS (MAHAYANA), VISIONARIES (INCLUDING HEARERS OF VOICES), MYSTICS (EXCLUDING QUANTUM PHYSICISTS), ANARCHISTS. There were many more.

Virgilia sighed deeply as we gazed at the sign. 'This module gives us no end of trouble,' she said. 'Why?' I asked. 'It all looks very well organized to me.' 'The trouble is,' she said, 'we have to keep subdividing the sects. No sooner do we think we've got one lot sorted out than a schism turns up somewhere else.' 'Because of doctrinal differences, you mean?' 'Doctrinal disputes are tolerable within a certain vocabulary level,' she explained. 'It's when the lexical differentiation factor is greater than 25 per 100 that we have to begin to subdivide.' As we stood talking, two men in overalls, armed with hammer and nails, marched up and fixed two more arms to the already groaning signpost. These read: SOCIAL AND LIBERAL DEMOCRATS and DEMOCRATIC AND SOCIAL LIBERALS. 'See what I mean?' said Virgilia, with an air of resignation, as we started off on our temple tour.

The vast temple was subdivided into a multiplicity of tiny private chapels, each with its own unique architectural style, and each separated from the others by ornately carved screens, barbed wire and armed security guards. 'Unfortunately,' said Virgilia, rounding us all up, 'there isn't time to see everything. But I'll give you each one of these admission voucher packs. They enable you to go into up to twenty chapels of your choice free of charge. Just tear off a ticket from the pack and give it to the guard at the entrance and he'll let you in. I'll give you this booklet as well, *Babel Beliefs and Cults: a brief guide* and that should help you to find your way around. I'll be waiting for you at the temple entrance, where we came in. Is three hours enough? Fine. Oh, one last thing, when you go into the chapels, please observe the religious customs there. These people take their beliefs very seriously, so please respect them. Do not mock them and take special care not to disagree with any of the worshippers. It could cause offence and in some cases it could lead to a very nasty incident. You shouldn't need to speak with any of the devotees, but if you do you will find some useful phrases in the relevant section of the guide booklet.' She set off for the main entrance, and we, clutching our guide books and admission vouchers, departed in different directions, according to inclination. I found myself so anxious to avoid Klaus that I ended up on my own. He is very informative, but somehow it's difficult to think your own thoughts when he's around. It's a bit like being on holiday with a history textbook.

I spent a very pleasant few hours wandering round the different chapels and drinking in the atmosphere. I visited one temple consecrated to nature gods where pictures of seals and whales and trees decorated the walls, and another dedicated to a matriarchal cult where women in various stages of pregnancy were involved in devotional breathing rites. I attended one ceremony where everyone sat on the ground in silence and another where everyone lay on the floor and screamed. I draped a shawl over my head to attend one rite and took off all my clothes to participate in another. In one chapel I put some money in a box as it was passed round; in another I wrote a cross on a piece of paper and put it in a box as I walked out. I met one sage who predicted that since my moon was in Mercury I would enter a time of prosperity and harmony when my instincts were to be trusted, and another who prophesied universal doom in the form of raging all-consuming fire followed by the dark night of a nuclear winter.

I learnt about birth, rebirth, pre-birth, afterbirth and the afterlife. I tried to understand the nature of Big Bangs and Small Communities, Deep Ecology and Higher Consciousness. I learnt how to release my essential self through Pre-creation Therapy, Body Electronics, Primal Screaming, Early-morning Jogging and Voting Liberal. I picked up pamphlets on Tri-polar Energy Fields and Planetary Focal Points, on Organic Gardening and Self-Development, on Karmic Life Trends and Inbeaming Light Energy Codings, on Naked Singularities and Releasing Guilt and Negative Ambition. I listened to lectures on Sub-atomic Particles and Nuclear Families, on Vegetarian Cookery and Assertiveness Training, on Indian Medicine Wheel Teachings and the Proletarian Revolution. Finally I sat through a lengthy sermon on Getting on the Right Wavelength to God (but I've forgotten whether this was in the Methodist, the Radio Hams or the Quantum Mechanics chapel).

Most of all, though, I gave money. Every chapel seemed to have a good cause to support, and I gave donations to miners' wives and battered husbands, to the League for Retired Structuralists and to a Rest Home for Distressed Quantum Physicists. I contributed to research into the Aquarian Triangle, the Bermuda Triangle and the Eternal Triangle. I put money towards a Roof Restoration Fund in the Baptist church and a Shaky Foundation Repair Fund in the Social Democrat chapel. I paid for a ride on the Spiritualist Ghost Train, the Socialist Rollercoaster and all the swings and roundabouts of the various liberal and social democratic parties. I even braved the Quantum Leap (35 baubels) and the Paradigm Shift (25 baubels). I had my biorhythms and astral configurations mapped, and communicated with a sixteenth-century fisherman on Astral Plane 9 who said he knew my grandma's ghost and she was doing fine. I wrote my name on a brick in the Chapel of the Higher Self, and bought booklets on Bringing God into your Life, Grand Unification Energy, Experiencing the Equinox and the Early Life of Trotsky.

I tried my best to communicate with the different religious groups by looking up appropriate phrases in *Babel Beliefs and Cults*. I greeted one sect with 'God Save the Whale', another with 'May your planet always be ascendant', and a third with 'Hope it never comes to the Big Crunch'. I mumbled '*Shantih, shantih*' in one chapel and 'Come the Revolution' in another. I addressed one group as 'Brothers', another group as 'Sisters' and a third as 'Friends'. I learnt phrases such as 'brotherhood of man', 'the peace of God', 'the synergy of trust' and 'the dictatorship of the proletariat', and had it revealed to me not only that 'every state in space has a definite probability', but also that 'the Great Starfleet Ashram of the Office of Christ is now situated over the Global Heart Wheel.'

Finally, when I had used up all my tickets and was getting tired and thinking of rejoining Virgilia at the entrance, I caught sight of a sign in carved stonework above an arched doorway. CafE, said the letters amid curling stone tendrils and plump stone cherubs. I decided to go in for a cup of tea, but was stopped at the door by the security guard, who demanded my ticket. I was surprised that you needed a ticket for a café and told him that all I wanted was a cup of tea. The guard started to laugh and explained that the 'a' in the sign was really an 'o' with a stray tendril curling round it. I said that to me it didn't really matter too much how they spelt it but I was happy to settle for a coffee if they didn't have any tea. The guard was nearly speechless with laughter at his own private joke, but managed to gasp out, 'Oh no, you'll get tea in there all right. They know how to make tea all right in there. Just remember not to swear, and to stick your little finger out when you hold the cup. And don't be surprised if you get a cucumber sandwich with it. Or maybe you'd prefer a glass of wine and a little wafer.' And, still panting with laughter, he stood back to let me in.

I must admit the decor in the teashop did surprise me a little. It wasn't exactly cosy, but the stone carving and stained glass were very tastefully done, and I suppose it was all in keeping with the atmosphere of the temple to have a Theme Café. They might have turned the heating up a bit though – with all that stone around it was absolutely freezing – and I thought it was a bit over the top to have all the waiters dressed in cassocks and dog collars. I sat down on a high backed carved wooden bench and summoned one of the waiters who was hanging around the top table. He seemed strangely surprised at my request, but when I told him I was exhausted and absolutely parched, he said he'd see what the bishop's wife could come up with. He came back in a few minutes and said that the bishop's wife had the kettle on and if I'd like to go over to the palace I could have tea with the Mothers' Union.

The palace was a cavernous, shabby, draughty house where I sat on a large plump flowery chintz covered sofa, holding my bone china teacup in one hand and my triangular crustless cucumber sandwich in the other, and listening to the chatter of a roomful of large plump flowery chintz covered ladies. The decor reminded me rather of the Middle Floor house where we had played dinnerparty games, but no one here was playing any games and I didn't understand much of the conversation, which was all about who was to arrange the flowers in time for Matins and the new crèche rota for Family Service and whether the sexton's wife's skirts were a little too short for Sunday school and why the new verger was always late for Evensong and what the two choirboys had been up to in the sacristy before Sung Eucharist and whether the Thursday Sitting Group could be prevailed upon to embroider some new hassocks.

I was wondering if they knew any good dinnerparty games and debating with myself whether to ask them if they could teach me how to play Inter-course Intercourse, when the door opened and in came the bishop, divesting himself of his cassock as he entered. 'Good afternoon everyone, bless you all,' he intoned sonorously, beaming round the assembled company, and helping himself to tea and Victoria sponge. Smiling benignly, he looked round for somewhere to sit and his gaze alighted on me. 'Ah, a new sheep joins the fold,' he said jovially, and came across to sit next to me. I explained hurriedly that I wasn't a new sheep but a tourist who had drifted into his church by accident and unfortunately couldn't join his fold because I had to rejoin my tour group. 'Too bad, too bad,' he said, biting into the sponge cake, and added, 'What do you think of the Tower so far then?' I said politely that I had found the Middle Floors very quaint and picturesque and that I was looking forward to seeing the Top Floor tomorrow.

At that, he became suddenly rather morose and, putting down his sponge cake, heaved a sigh and said, 'We used to be the Top Floor religion you know.' 'Really?' I said politely with half an eye on the clock. 'Yes,' he went on, sipping tea reflectively. 'Pillar of the Establishment and all that. National heroes buried in our cathedrals. State funerals for Prime Ministers. Royal weddings. Televised services at Christmas and Easter. You even got the odd Cabinet minister going to his local constituency church sometimes.' 'What happened? And what's the Top Floor religion now?' 'Well, we rather exceeded our brief. Overstepped the mark a bit. We should have known really. There were precedents in history. Look what happened to Thomas à Becket. Or Thomas More for that matter. We forgot the ground rules. Don't argue with the ruling party. And don't examine your conscience in public. Setting up soup kitchens to feed the poor and taking calf's foot jelly to the sick is one thing. That's playing a constructive role in society. Suggesting that there's too much poverty around or that the sick might be better off in hospital is quite another. That's meddling in politics. We should have stuck to running Adventure Playgrounds on bomb sites instead of commenting in the media on inner-city deprivation.'

'So what happened to you?' 'Well, first the Government told us to keep to our own patch, which was Public Morality and Spiritual Welfare and to leave politics to them. Then they decided we weren't doing too good a job on Public Morality and Spiritual Welfare either, and that they'd better take that over too and incorporate it into politics. So we got demoted. Now we're just a sect like all the others. No access to the media. No influence on the public. Haven't done a State funeral for years. Let alone a royal wedding.' 'So what's the Top Floor religion now? What god do they worship?' The bishop set down his teacup. An impish gleam came into his eyes. 'Well,' he said, 'I think they've rather lost sight of a god. But they do worship Large Prophets.'

'But,' I said to Virgilia when we met her at the entrance, 'some of the languages I heard in the chapels today were not entirely new to me.' 'Where have you heard them before?' asked Virgilia, looking worried. 'Well, in Hobby Hour I overheard some phrases that sounded very like the languages used in the Environmentalist chapel or in the Psychotherapy confessional, and in the Education sector some of the words I heard sounded as if they could have been Leftist vocabulary.'

Virgilia cheered up. 'Oh, that's all right,' she said. 'Lexical infiltration of Education is potentially disturbing, I agree, but as you've seen, we've more or less dealt with that problem. As for Hobby Hour, that's nothing serious. Sometimes people will pick up the odd word or phrase in another language. It doesn't mean they can speak the language or really understand the culture and the ideas behind it. Just because you can say *pizza* or *spaghetti* doesn't mean you can speak Italian does it? It just makes you sound knowledgeable. It's like that on the Middle Floors. People like to sound knowledgeable, so they throw in the odd foreign word occasionally. Particularly in Hobby Hour. Middle Floor people like to sound exotic or esoteric. It's a status thing. It doesn't mean they seriously believe in, or even understand the ideas behind the language. They just like the aura it gives them. There's all the difference in the world between a Belief and a hobby and as a rule Middle Floor people don't really go in for Belief. They prefer hobbies. So although we can't entirely get rid of lexical cross-contamination, as I said before it's only when the density of lexical variation reaches 25 per 100 that we have to start worrying.'

Virgilia herself was beginning to worry at this point, as several of the tour group had not yet returned and a Sectwatchman had to be dispatched in search of them. He eventually returned with two in tow, whom he had managed to detach from the Second Coming of Aquarius Holy Chakra sect, but confessed failure in the case of Tomas, an elderly German businessman who had joined the Grailwatchers, and Annette, a Dutch housewife, who had become a Social Democrat.

Babel, 25 May, morning

I had become so fascinated by what I had seen in the temple that I had completely forgotten my appointment with Mystery Woman as I called her to myself. I remembered with a shock as we all trooped into the hotel that evening. 'I've got a bit of a headache,' I told the others. 'I think I'll skip dinner and lie down for a bit.' Dorothy was very sympathetic, and declared that Religion always gave her a headache too, but declining her ministrations and Klaus's offer of an extremely efficacious German medicine, I went up to my room, waited till they had all dispersed, then slipped out of the hotel, leaving a DO NOT DISTURB sign on the door of my room. Before I left I grabbed up a pile of papers in the hope that this would make me look vaguely academic. They were mainly brochures and leaflets, but I put some sheets of paper and my notebook on the top and hoped that this would do.

My mood had changed since the night before. I now felt not a shred of my original curiosity. I merely felt angry with myself for getting involved in this complicated and unnecessary affair. This was a problem I didn't need, didn't want, and I wished it would go away. By the time I reached the girl's door, I was out of breath and extremely grumpy. I mentally rehearsed a short speech in which I would tell her to stop playing silly games, and that I wanted nothing more to do with her or her charter, took a deep breath and knocked on the door.

No one answered. I knocked again. Still no reply. My overwhelming emotion was relief, though to my surprise there was a part of me that felt somehow cheated and vaguely disappointed. I had turned to go when a figure came scurrying along the corridor and approached me. It was the Professor of Medicine. He laid a finger to his lips and led me into the room. 'But where's . . .' I began. He nodded sadly. 'I'm afraid she's been Cut,' he said. 'Cut?' 'Yes. They came for her this morning.' 'Who came?' 'Incpol.' 'Do you mean some kind of Secret Police?' 'Oh no, they're not at all secret. They get a lot of publicity. Anyway here's the Charter.' He laid a sealed envelope on the desk. But I was still worried about the girl. 'What has happened to her? Were the cuts bad? Will she die?' I imagined her swathed in bandages, a silent white form on a hospital bed. He shook his head. 'No, of course she won't die. But the cuts were quite severe, yes. In fact the whole department was axed.' I was speechless. Images of severed limbs and beheaded professors, of book-lined walls spattered with blood, ran through my head. I had not imagined that such barbarities could still go on in a civilized country.

The more I thought about it, the more I realized I did not want to know. I shut the images out of my mind. 'Look,' I said, firmly. 'I'd like to help you. But it's not my country and I don't feel it's my business. I'm just a tourist. I don't even know what this charter is.' He looked surprised. 'But I thought you knew all that,' he said. 'After all, you brought the message.' I explained what had happened in the Basement and told him the story of the disaffected computer.

At this he looked extremely grave. 'I'm sorry,' he said. 'We thought you were a member of the Movement and that the message meant you would take the Charter to the Top for us.' 'What did you want me to do with it?' 'Well, publicize it,' he said vaguely. 'Spread the word around. Get them to take some notice of it. After all, it is signed by most of us here on the Middle Floors.' 'But can't you do that yourselves?' I asked. 'It seems a bit unfair to involve me.' The Professor sighed. 'I agree,' he said. 'It's nothing to do with you really. But it's impossible for us to get access to the Top Floor. You can't get an entry permit. They speak a different language. And there are no channels for communication in this direction. Top down only is the rule. If only you knew . . .'

But I had already heard more than I wanted to know. I was a tourist not a secret agent. I didn't want to know about this society's seamy realities. I had paid a good deal of money to come on this trip and I was determined to enjoy myself. Besides, in the pre-departure orientation talk they had warned us never to accept packets from strangers. I communicated all this to the Professor, regretted that I could not help him, wished him success with his enterprise, shook hands, picked up my papers from the desk, and walked rapidly back to the hotel, where everyone was packing up for the lift to the Top Floor.

It was not until I had regained my room and begun to pack my things that I realized the awful truth. The envelope containing the charter was in my possession. I must have picked it up from the desk, together with my papers, in my haste to leave. Or, the suspicion crossed my mind, perhaps the Professor had slipped it in among them when I was not looking.

I sat down on the floor cushion in my room and tried to take stock of the situation. I was an innocent tourist enjoying a much-needed holiday from a demanding job. All I wanted was relaxation and a change of scene. So how was it that I now had in my possession a mysterious and possibly illegal document from a secretive and possibly illegal organization that I was to deliver – to whom, I didn't know? How did I get myself into this mess? I am always interested in how people in other cultures live their lives, but I never wanted to know *this* much about it. This was ruining my holiday. This was where my stupid curiosity had led me. I wanted to *see* what life in this country was like: I didn't want to become a part of it. I decided to have nothing more to do with the whole idiotic enterprise. I would tear the envelope and its contents up and throw them away. But something made me stop short of doing this. The document would make an unusual souvenir, I reasoned to myself. It would be a good talking point: the episode would make an interesting anecdote when I got back. So I folded the envelope in half, tucked it away carefully between the layers of pullovers and handkerchiefs in my suitcase, and retired to bed for a night of confused and uneasy dreams.

Our lift has just been called and is boarding now, so I'll have to sign off here. I must say I'm looking forward to the Top Floor. It's all been very picturesque here, but I've had enough of intrigue and herb teas – and the thought of another night on one of those cotton mattresses you roll out on the floor is more than I can bear!

The Top Floor

Babel, 25 May, evening

I was rather surprised when Virgilia said goodbye to us before we caught the lift up here, since I'd assumed she'd be with us for the whole trip. But she had to meet another tour group arriving at the Ground Floor tomorrow, so we have a new guide, a young girl with short blow-dried blonde hair, and a peaches-and-cream complexion. She's quite pretty actually – an improvement on Virgilia, anyway – but has rather large teeth and a very unfortunate laugh, which I was treated to when I tried pronouncing her name. 'Oh, no,' she said, with a loud bray. 'It's pronounced the Italian way. Mummy and Daddy had their honeymoon in Florence, and I was the little souvenir they brought back with them. Bit of excess baggage on the way home, Daddy always said.' And she neighed with laughter again. 'But,' she added kindly, 'if it's too difficult for you to pronounce, you can shorten it. Just call me Richie – all my friends do.'

Richie met us at the liftport and took us into The City. I'll never forget my first sight of the massed skyscrapers in the distance, glinting and sparkling in the noonday sun. It looked to me like a magic city, its towers created out of gold and pearl and silver, though Rick said Hong Kong or New York were far more impressive. Rick has begun to get on my nerves lately. He collects countries like other people collect stamps. I tried to ignore him, and as we sped towards the centre along the pleasant tree-lined avenues where walls and high hedges hid large estates from view, and iron gateways offered occasional glimpses of stone or half-timbered mansions, I found myself wondering what kind of people lived here and what they had done to earn this fairytale existence.

I put the question to Richie, who considered it thoughtfully, her china-blue eyes wide open and her rosebud mouth slightly parted. 'I don't know,' she said at length. 'I've never really thought about it that way before. It just sort of *is* like that. It's the way things are.' Despite this explanation, I wanted to find out more about the inhabitants, so opened my *Government of Babel Tourist Handbook* for further illumination. However, it said more or less the same thing: 'All modular units,' it explained, 'have their own appointed site in the Tower.' What I really wanted to know was who appointed the sites. But all was explained when we approached the monumental arch that was the gateway to The City. An elaborately carved inscription decorated the top of the arch. 'God,' it informed me, 'made them high or lowly, and ordered their estate.'

We drove along boulevards where gleaming plate-glass and steel towers alternated with rows of tall houses where flights of stone steps swept up to imposing doorways and eventually came to our hotel, housed in one of the glass and steel towers. 'Just time for a quick freshen-up now,' said Richie. 'Don't spend too long. There's a super new little place just opened round the corner and I've booked us all in for lunch.'

The new little place was called Palettes and was decorated inside in pastel shades of pink and mushroom. The walls were lined with mirrors with ornate Florentine frames. I found it rather disconcerting to be eating opposite myself and asked Richie whether it was a Top Floor custom to dine out with yourself. 'I don't know,' she said, considering it thoughtfully, 'I've never thought of it like that before. It's true, there are a lot of restaurants with mirrors . . .' She was interrupted by a polite cough from the proprietor who was settling us all into our seats. 'You will find that most of the better restaurants have mirrors,' he said. 'It's so that even if you are sitting facing the wall you can keep an eye on who is coming and going. And they of course can see you. Eating out in one of the better restaurants would be a bit of a waste of time if no one saw you doing it, wouldn't it?'

I was further disconcerted when the menu arrived and I found I was expected to choose my food not by taste but by colour. The menu, designed like an artist's palette, offered a choice between the Red Menu (vivid splashes of crimson and scarlet to create a mood of warmth and goodwill), the Green Menu (cool shades of lime and leaf-bud: a refreshing choice for a summer's day), the Brown Menu (subtly varied shades of beige and caramel soothe and satisfy) and the Pink-and-White Menu (fresh and delicate tones of rose-pink and coolest white harmonize perfectly to offer an ambiance of pure delight). This last description appealed to me most, so I chose the Pink-and-White Menu. The waiter whisked away the colour chart and reappeared in a trice with a trayful of drinks and booklets. To me he presented a glass of pink champagne and a small booklet where white italic handwriting adorned petal-pink pages. The others got aperitifs of whisky, chartreuse or burgundy, accompanied by appropriately coloured pamphlets. Obviously we had a lot of reading to get through before the hors-d'oeuvres. I opened my book and began to read about my dinner.

I spent a very instructive twenty minutes or so before the first course arrived, reading up the background to my meal. All the ingredients had been thoroughly researched and I now know a good deal more about the life-cycle of the salmon, the history of the strawberry and methods of curing ham than I did when I started. The arrival of the waiters jolted me out of a very interesting paragraph about the medicinal uses of vanilla pods, and I hurriedly turned to the back page where a kind of poem had been written, describing what I was about to eat. It made lengthy reading, as every dish was described twice, first briefly in French followed by a longer, more lyrical translation.

A short introduction informed me that 'The chef was inspired in his creation of this menu by Chinese Tang dynasty paintings of plum blossom. The sequence of the dishes in this fresh spring-like menu reflects the progress of the plum blossoms from tightly curled buds to snowy drifts of petals on the frosty ground.' My first course was described as: '*Mousse de jambon et endive en floraison, sauce pastèque.*' Reading the translation, I learned that 'The delicate flavours of spring-cured Tuscan ham and crisp snow-white endives cultivated in the Provençal foothills, combine together unforgettably in this fragrantly spiced mousse, given an extra piquancy by the subtle addition of watermelon sauce.'

Looking down at the table, I discovered, in the centre of my large white bone china plate, a small pink blossom made out of mousse and garnished with a leaf or two cut out of watermelon. It did not take me long to eat this and I waited hungrily for the next course. I was surprised when it arrived to discover that it too consisted of a small pink mousse-textured blossom, though this time accompanied by leaves made from mashed potato and buds cut from radishes. I leafed through my menu to discover what I was about to eat, and found that this was '*Rosette de mousseline de saumon, sauce framboise, garni de feuilles de pommes et radis.*' My last plate ('*Purée de fraises et choufleur en pétales, coulis de champagne et cassis*') had only a few delicately-tinted pink petals strewn on its white surface. I was on the whole, though, quite glad I'd chosen this menu, when I saw the others faced with small heart-shaped moulds of raw beef and red cabbage or leafy patterns of avocado, dill and gooseberry. I would have liked a coffee at the end of the meal, but the waiter expressed such horror that I had to settle for rose-hip tea, which was served with two squares of Turkish Delight and a handful of crystallized rose-petals.

Perhaps it was something to do with the composition of the food on the plates that now brought a question to my mind. It struck me that during the five days we had spent so far in Babel, we had not done any of the usual tourist things such as visiting art galleries. Ignoring Hugo and Rosamund, who were wrangling over who should have the last square of chocolate, I turned to Richie, who was having an animated conversation with the Italian at the end of the table, and tried to attract her attention. 'We haven't seen any Babel art galleries or museums yet,' I began, when I finally managed to catch her eye. 'Would it be possible to visit one or two in the next few days?' Richie looked a little blank. 'I don't know,' she said thoughtfully. 'I haven't thought about it. I've never been to one myself. In fact I don't even know if there *are* any.' She brightened up a little. 'Let's ask Jason. He'll know: he's *frightfully* artistic.'

She dispatched one of the waiters to fetch the proprietor from the kitchen, and a few moments later Jason came out, untying his apron and smoothing back his hair. Impeccably dressed in a crisp pink linen suit and beige silk shirt, he harmonized beautifully with his restaurant. 'Is there a little problemette, sweetheart?' he said, drawing up a chair next to Richie. 'Hold forth. I'm all ears.' 'Art galleries,' said Richie, fixing her big blue eyes on him. 'Museums. Where would I find one? You know how dreadfully dim I am about things like that.' Jason threw back his head and laughed. (I've never seen anyone do that before.) 'Art galleries!' he said. 'Where have *you* been for the last decade, ducky? There aren't any any more.' 'Oh well,' said Richie comfortably. 'That explains why I've never been to one.' 'What happened to them?' I asked. 'Act of Parliament about ten years ago,' said Jason. 'And hey presto, all privatized. Happened in the twinkling of an eye. Two shakes of a duck's arse. And there you were. Or there you weren't, rather.'

I still didn't understand. 'But what difference does it make whether they're private or state-owned? You can still go to them can't you?' 'Oh no you can't, dearie,' said Jason, 'because there isn't a "them" to go to any more. It isn't exactly the museums that were privatized. It was more like the little bits and pieces inside them.' I began to see what he meant. 'You mean that they sold off the exhibits?' 'Ooh, you're a quick one! No fooling you, is there? Yes, sweetie, you caught my drift. Hit the nail right on the head.' I wondered whether to feel indignant. 'But that's outrageous,' I hazarded, 'selling off the nation's heirlooms.' 'Oh, it isn't really,' said Jason soothingly. 'It's quite logical when you think about it. Art is the expression of the individual spirit in its highest form. It's got no business being state property. It was always intended to be by the individual for the individual. Here in Babel we believe that the State has no business interfering in Art.'

For a moment he had sounded uncannily like Virgilia, and I was quite relieved when he went on, 'Besides, what did the State do with all its little heirloomettes? Stuck them up in rows on blank white walls or shoved them inside glass cases. That's no way to treat a work of art. Art abuse, I call it. No, a work of art has to have a sympathetic environment. Walls painted the right colour. Carpets and curtains that pick out the dominant tones. The right shade of sofa. That kind of thing.' He paused and then went on, 'And another thing. It's hardly cost-effective to keep works of art in museums, is it? Doesn't make financial sense. It's a bit like keeping all your nest-eggs in the bank when they could be out and earning you money on the market. Mustn't hide your assets under a bushel now, must you? I ask you, is there any other industry that manufactures products and then keeps them under glass cases for people to gawp at?' I had to admit he was right.

'But what about contemporary art?' I pursued. 'What's the art scene in Babel now?' 'No getting you off the subject is there?' said Jason. 'Right little limpet aren't we? Well, most of the serious artists, like yours truly, old Humbleself here for example, have diversified. That means,' he went on hurriedly, before I could open my mouth, 'finding new forms of expression for our artistic talents. Some have gone into Int Dec, of course, or Property Development. Some are in Fashion or Furniture. But a good many of us have opened restaurants. Food is where it's at at the moment, artistically speaking.'

'So what are the current trends? What are the new movements?' This promised to be an exciting conversation. 'Foodwise, Abstract Expressionism is still going strong, but the Minimalist movement is dead as a dodo now. The punters didn't really get off on Hyper-Realism either. They wanted to eat the food, not just look at a photo of it. And I think they were right: food should be a multi-media experience. You're dealing on several planes at once here. Colour, shape and pattern aren't enough. You've got to get into tactility. Texture. Taste. That's what makes it such an exciting medium to work with.'

'And what about yourself?' I can't tell you how thrilled I was to be sitting there discussing the Babel art world with one of its leading lights. 'I first made my name in Colour Field food, and I think you can still see that influence in my work. But just recently I've rediscovered a wealth of meaning in Representational food. Symbol and allegory play a large part in my work now. And I've started to go right back and take my inspiration from the ancients. I'm very influenced by Classical Chinese ink drawing and Ancient Egyptian art at the moment. I think they have a lot to tell us. The latest thing of course is food sculpture. People are beginning to realize that we haven't been fully exploiting the three-dimensional nature of the material we work with. It's just in its infancy, of course, but I find the whole thing tremendously exciting. I think it could be really big.'

'I'd be fascinated,' I said, 'to see more of what's going on in Babel.' 'Artwise,' I added. I was beginning to catch on to the lingo. 'Well,' said Jason, 'what are you doing this afternoon? Richie, baby, what have you got up your sleevelet for our friends today?' 'I don't know really,' said Richie, tossing a blonde curl out of her eyes. 'I haven't thought about it. A spot of shopping maybe. Dinner at Collage. Could go to the Insider Dealers concert. Finish up at the Topboss Club?' 'Would you be very angry with me,' asked Jason, 'if I expropriated one of your little charges for the afternoon? Meet up again for drinky-poos at the Topboss? Then we could go to Artco and Litbiz together,' he explained to me, 'and you'd get your little peepette at the cultural scenerama.'

In the end, five of us went. Klaus came, of course. Dorothy declared she'd always been one for the arts, and Miranda who had been feeling at a loose end since Tracey had taken up with one of the Spaniards, came too. Finally, Hugo, who was having a bit of a lovers' tiff with Rosamund, decided to join us, while Rosamund stalked off sulkily with the others.

Artco was a very stimulating experience. Miranda and I admired Minimalist sofas, neo-cubist garlic crushers and designer vegetables, and Jason chatted knowledgeably with artware manufacturers and buyers who wanted an artwork that would reflect the mood of their green satin curtains and pick up some of the themes in the kelim rug, while Hugo and Klaus wrangled about neo-expressionist influences on artichoke design.

The avant-garde department excited me most. It was here that the newest ideas were to be found, at the forefront of artistic development. At first I was surprised to see no paintings, nor any evidence of artistic activity at all. Instead, some of the artists were busy scribbling lengthy tracts on reams of paper, while others contemplatively sucked their pencils and after a good deal of thought wrote long numbers on small slips of paper. 'The canvas has been completely superseded, of course,' whispered Jason. 'Art exists, if at all, as a concept in the mind of the buyer.' 'Do you mean there's no work of art?' 'On the ball today aren't we? Hole in one.' 'You mean there's nothing there at all?' 'There's no holding you back is there? The work of art as a tangible presence is of course completely *passé* these days. It's the *idea* of the work of art that's significant. Non-existent art was the only logical step after non-representational art.' 'So what are they writing?' I whispered back. 'Some of them are writing expositions of the theory behind their art-concept.' 'And the others?' 'Well, some of them believe that art needs no introduction. The artist should communicate directly with his patron through the Artwork.' 'So what are they writing?' I whispered. 'Price tags,' Jason hissed back.

After Artco, the others departed. Dorothy's feet were killing her, so Miranda took her off in search of a decent cup of tea and Hugo was feeling too gloomy to take any further interest in the excursion, so Klaus accompanied him back to the hotel. Jason and I continued on to Litbiz.

Litbiz was housed in the building next to Artco, and was just as fascinating in its own way. When we arrived some kind of party was in progress. Champagne flowed freely and various artistic-looking figures in cream suits and silk shirts nibbled caviar canapés. The air was alive with the hum of malicious gossip and the rustling of paper as contracts were signed in corners. 'What's going on?' I asked Jason. 'Lunch,' he said, briefly. 'There's always one going on here.' I was introduced to a sleek young man in a striped shirt and loose trousers. 'This is the designer,' said Jason. He and Jason then engaged in a strange ritual. They stood opposite each other a little way apart, smiling broadly and nodding their heads up and down, but did not once meet each other's eyes. Instead, as they exchanged a few words, they gazed fixedly over each other's shoulders, their eyes moving backwards and forwards as they scanned the other guests. At almost exactly the same moment they both exclaimed, 'Fescinating. Ebsolutely. Terribly sorry. Do excuse me for a moment. Just seen Cynthia. Ebsolutely must have a word.' 'Fescinating to chet with you,' said the designer politely to me as he left.

When he had gone I asked Jason, 'Who was he? And what did he design?' 'The book, of course,' said Jason, making his way purposefully towards a waiter with a tray of champagne. 'What book?' 'The book that's being launched of course,' said Jason, capturing a glass and making for the canapés. I looked around. 'What book is it? And is the author here?' 'Author?' said Jason vaguely, securing a handful of canapés and heading for the smoked salmon. 'The writer,' I said, trailing behind him. 'The one who wrote the book.' 'You *are* behind the times. What a quaint little country *you* must come from! These days books aren't written. They're designed.' 'Designed?' 'Take a look,' said Jason. 'There's a pile of them over there.'

I wandered over to where a display of brightly-coloured books stood on a table, and leafed through one. I got a surprise. The pages were completely blank. I rejoined Jason at the satay tray and demanded, 'Why are all the pages blank?' 'They always are,' said Jason, 'these days.' I had a sudden insight. 'Is it like Artworks? The concept has superseded the object?' 'Oh, no,' said Jason, tucking into an asparagus roulade, 'On the contrary. Just the opposite.' I could not understand this at all, and somewhere between the vol-au-vents and the prawn toast he explained to me patiently, 'Look, a book is a product, like anything else. It's an object. You have to sell it. And like everything else, sales depend on presentation. Profile. Image. Content is irrelevant. Most people don't read the books they buy. They buy them because they've been persuaded that they ought to have them. The next step is logical really. If content is irrelevant, why bother to have it? It's expensive and unnecessary. It cut production costs quite substantially to eliminate the author. And no one really noticed.'

Several canapés later, we left the lunch and went on to dinner at the Square Meal (a cubist restaurant). But on our way to join the others at the Topboss Club, we passed in front of Litbiz. A tip-up truck was parked in the courtyard, disgorging its load into a chute in the wall. The load consisted of hundreds of the brightly-coloured books I had seen at the lunch.

'What's happening to the books?' I asked. 'Pulping,' said Jason shortly. I was aghast. 'But it was only published this afternoon.' 'The shelf-life of books is very limited these days,' said Jason. 'I wouldn't worry about it. There'll be another one tomorrow.' But I couldn't put the thought out of my mind so easily. 'What about literature? What about all your great writers? Milton? Wordsworth? Dickens? Pope? Have they been pulped too?' 'Never heard of them,' said Jason easily. 'Probably exceeded their sell-by date.' 'But don't you have any places where copies of the classics are kept? Where people can borrow them?' 'Libelries, do you mean?' said Jason. 'They were all closed down. 1995. Bringing Truth From Error Act.' I was at first appalled. 'That's terrible. That's destroying your heritage. It's like censorship of the past.' Jason laughed. 'Firstly,' he said, 'it was uneconomic to keep those places open. No one ever read the books except for exams. And when literature became an economically unviable subject, no one read the books at all. And then, many of the books contained potentially dangerous misinformation. If you'd read some of them, for example, you might have got the idea that Babel was famous for its fogs, or that some of the inhabitants looked like horses, or that we never gave people second helpings of dinner, or that the Secret Services were up to all kinds of illegal things. The right to the truth is a fundamental human freedom, and the Government has to ensure that every citizen is protected from misinformation.' I had to admit the logic of his argument.

We had now reached the club and, on entering it, I was rather taken aback by the decor. The bare floorboards had holes in them, the walls were covered unevenly with yellowing paint, or pasted with strips of peeling wallpaper, and the windows were hung with grimy shreds of net curtain. I was surprised to find that Richie patronized a place like this and said as much to Jason. 'Why don't they do it up?' I asked. Jason laughed. 'Sweetie,' he said, 'Derelict is chic. The Eighties Inner City Look is the latest in nostalgia. The Deprivation Experience is cool these days. And besides,' he went on, 'the place *is* done up. They spent a couple of hundred grand on getting it to look like this. It must have taken hours of rag-rubbing to achieve the special effect on the walls. And the curtains are hand-ripped.'

I looked around me with new respect. The room was filled with people, dancing, drinking, or screeching at each other. Everyone was dressed with the same startling originality. The men wore faded overalls, patched and torn trousers, or old coats that were much too big for them. The girls were in shapeless dresses and stained cardigans. Some wore fluffy slippers and curlers. Jason followed my glance. 'Designer poverty,' he said. 'The latest look.' 'What kind of people come here?' I asked. 'Oh, they're mainly in the creative *métiers*,' said Jason vaguely. 'Do excuse me for a moment. I've just seen some people I know, and I really ought to have a little mingle.'

He disappeared into the crowd. I could dimly see Richie at the end of the room, wearing a print housecoat and headscarf. She was dancing with the Italian. Rosamund and Tracey were with the Spaniards. I went over to the bar where Rick and Klaus were intellectualizing loudly. Klaus usually gets the upper hand in these discussions. Rick has been to more countries, but Klaus knows more words. The debate seemed to be getting acrimonious, so I joined Hugo, who had just ordered his third whisky. He was not very stimulating company, so I decided to try to mingle with the natives. I met with no success. The first group I joined were engrossed in some sort of private game, involving much scribbling in black leather notebooks. The dialogue I overheard went like this: '11 at Snoops?' 'Sorry, no good.' '12 at Scoffers then?' 'Can't make 12. Can you do 1 at Splurge?' 'Make it 1.30?' It seemed to be some sort of betting game. I fared no better with the next group: 'His work has a striking verticality with a playful overlay of ethnicity, but I found the whole thing something of a constructional understatement,' said the first speaker. 'The fetishistic nuances *were* quite exciting,' agreed the second speaker, 'but wouldn't you agree that the cultural mismatch of tonalities produces aesthetic vertigo?' The last group was equally incomprehensible: 'Three month sterling opened at 88.6 for August delivery, but by the end of the day . . .' began one man.

I didn't wait to hear more. I sought out Jason, who

was playing the staring-over-shoulders game with a group of baby-faced youths in custom-torn jackets. 'Who are these creative people?' I said. 'What do they create? And what do I do? I can't understand a word of the language.' 'They're all arty types,' said Jason. 'And what they create is mainly money. Communication is easier than you think. You don't have to know the language. Basically, all you have to do is smile and agree. Nod your head two or three times and say "Yah" very slowly and significantly. Or you can try "Ebsolutely". But make it sound important. You've got to get the stress right.'

I tried this and met with surprising success. In fact, by the end of the evening, I thought I had cottoned on to enough of the lingo to have a shot at it myself. 'I've always found,' I hazarded, 'that debt futures have a striking verticality, with no more than a playful overlay of uncertainty.' I wasn't prepared for the effect of my statement. Ears pricked up. Silence fell. All eyes turned in my direction. Encouraged, I went on, 'But of course gilts are crisply contemporary and I find them tremendously exciting at the moment, though something of a constructional understatement.' My audience waited with bated breath. Summoning up all the new vocabulary I had acquired, I continued, 'And the takeover by western culture of oriental tonalities, though admittedly producing cultural vertigo at times, has created a dynamic stasis which could be tremendously enriching to anyone prepared to invest in . . .' I stopped. My audience had disappeared. 'Where have they all gone?' I asked Jason, who was standing next to me. 'Straight to their carphones, I imagine,' he said when he had stopped laughing.

We left the club shortly after this. Partly because I felt the time had come to escort Hugo home, and partly because Jason had decided that Derelict was now *passé*. A new group of people had entered the club, of whom he seemed rather disapproving. 'Why?' I asked, looking at them. 'I can't see any difference. They look exactly like everyone else in here.' 'Unfortunately,' said Jason, steering Hugo past the doorman, 'it's not enough just to have designer clothes. You need a designer personality.'

Babel, 26 May, morning

I don't quite know what made me get the charter out from my suitcase where I had packed it away, and put it in my pocket this morning. I rationalized it to myself as occupational therapy: if Richie was going to be such an unsatisfactory tour guide, I had better provide myself with a project to occupy my time. But if I am honest, I think it had something to do with a conversation I had with Miranda late last night in the hotel bar. I found myself telling her about my trip to the Basement, something I had not described to any of the others so far. As I recounted my experiences, the blank stares and bowed shoulders of the people in the queue came back to me so vividly that I found myself describing the people and the scenes that I encountered there in terms that I had not even voiced to myself. Miranda's round brown eyes grew even rounder as I talked and when I had finished, she said, 'Gosh. How wonderful! I do wish I could have been there. It all sounds so exotic!' I searched her face for signs of irony, but her upturned freckled face was without guile and the round eyes were entirely innocent. I felt suddenly unaccountably angry with her, and stomped off to bed in a huff, leaving poor Miranda, still perched on her barstool, looking hurt and baffled.

I spent a restless night, troubled by dreams in which I searched frantically for something shadowy and undefined, or ran from footsteps that pursued me down concrete corridors from which there was no exit. I woke feeling exhausted, battered and still seething with a nameless anger. It wasn't until I had showered and was casting around irritably for a clean pair of socks that the thought came to me: my anger was really directed against myself. For weren't my own reactions four days ago the same as Miranda's last night? And it was something to do with this realization that made me snatch up the document from its hiding place and stuff it into my jacket pocket before going down to breakfast.

Breakfast this morning was a rather gloomy affair. Everyone seemed a little worse for wear after last night. I came down to a room steeped in silence. Hugo and Rosamund were glowering at each other from opposite ends of the table. Klaus and Rick had had a serious disagreement and Miranda whispered to me that Tracey and Dorothy had just had a full-scale row during which Tracey had called Dorothy a whiney old bag and Dorothy had replied that Tracey was a right little tart and that if she was her daughter she would put her across her knee and give her a good smackbottom. Only Richie was her usual self, immaculately groomed with not a hair out of place – indeed, she had already been to the hairdresser's that morning – though even she was a little quieter than normal. I think she's rather taken with the enigmatic Italian: they spent a long time gazing into each other's eyes over the *oeufs en cocotte à l'antillaise*.

I broke the silence by asking Richie what she had planned for us to do today. 'I don't know,' she replied, tearing her gaze away with difficulty from the brown eyes opposite hers. 'I haven't really thought about it. A spot of shopping maybe. Lunch at Dada's? . . .' She was rather rudely interrupted by Klaus who stated that he was not interested in shopping, but was writing an important paper on urban renewal and wanted particularly to see what was happening in the city centre, architecturally, and could she arrange, please, for an architectural tour, guided by an expert, please. Richie's china-blue eyes widened in alarm. 'I don't know much about architecture,' she said. 'In fact I don't know much about anything. I always have been awfully dim. But,' she said, brightening, 'Daddy is a property developer. He knows all about buildings. He could show you round. Or maybe one of the chaps in his office could help out. I'll arrange something.'

In the end Klaus, Dorothy and I opted for the City tour, and the rest went shopping. Even though they were still not on speaking terms, Hugo seemed determined not to leave Rosamund alone with the Spaniards again, and, to tell the truth, I was rather relieved that he wasn't coming as I was beginning to find his gloomy, brooding presence a little oppressive.

Daddy's office was on the 54th floor of a tall building that looked like a combination of a Greek temple and a refrigerator cooling system. The Corinthian columns soared up to the 66th floor where they were crowned with concrete capitals and a bas-relief frieze. Between the columns were acres of plate-glass and a complicated network of copper piping.

Daddy was too busy shouting figures down three phones at once, to talk to us, though he did give a courteous nod in our direction and passed us his card, which read:

PORTINARI PROPERTIES

Estate agents and property developers

Mortgages arranged 25%

Over his head, on the wall, a framed text read:

From him who would borrow of thee, turn not thou away.

Matthew 5, verse 42

One of his chaps had agreed to escort us round The City and show us what was going on property-wise, so we all four got into the glass-sided lift and sped down through the copper tubing to the ground floor.

Once outside, he and Klaus plunged into a learned discussion of the building we had just left. '. . . adds a new dimension to the reinterpretation of the role of the column.' '. . . subtly allusive . . .' '. . . plays with a pointed ambiguity on the sensibilities of the pseudo-purist . . .' '. . . witty and ironic comment on abstracted historicism . . .' they enthused.

I looked up at the tower. So it was really an enormous glass and concrete joke. It seemed rather permanent for a witticism. I wondered how many people were still sniggering behind their hands at the discomfiture of the pseudo-purists or chuckling over the wisecrack about abstracted historicism. Did the people who worked there still get a belly-laugh after ten years of entering the revolving doors at five-to-nine every morning?

Dorothy decided to enter the conversation at this point. 'I never did understand modern architecture,' she contributed. Daddy's chap looked at her with disdain. 'It isn't modern architecture,' he said. Dorothy looked a little crushed. We walked on and I saw her looking around at the steel and glass and concrete cubes and rectangles and rhomboids. It was a few blocks before she plucked up the courage to demand, 'Well, what is it if it isn't modern?' 'Post-modern,' said Daddy's chap briefly, and resumed his discussion with Klaus on urban renewal and real estate values.

We walked on down a street that sprouted slender stalks of steel and mirrored glass, and turned into another where concrete cubes were festooned with looped polythene tubing like tangled intestines. Glass pyramids and red-brick wigwams were interspersed with giant perspex bubbles and domes of lurid plastic. I saw teepees with gothic windows and igloos with Greek porticoes. Plastic funnels, concrete sails and steel rigging gave a nautical air to one building, while next door, Moorish arches, Byzantine domes, and Roman pillars lent a flourish to a concrete rhombus.

All the time I was straining my ears to follow the conversation. It was not easy to understand, but by listening hard I learnt quite a lot. I learnt, for example, that it was important to distinguish buildings that were post-modern from others that were ultra-modern, extra-modern, super-modern, or neo-modern. None seemed to be merely modern. I learnt about the New Brutalism and the New Objectivity, both of which seemed to be as old hat as being modern. I learnt about reductivists and revivalists, neo-plasticists and neo-classicists. I learnt about the theoretical significance of the slab and the different interpretations of the role of the portico, the archetypes of the shed and the hut and the ideology of rationalism. Most of all I learnt about the uses of irony, metaphor, ambiguity, lyricism, understatement, wit, allusion and quotation. By the end my head was aching. It seemed to me that you would need a degree in architecture just to know how to enter the door of one of these buildings. I was quite glad I didn't work in one. Every time I took the lift, I would be afraid I was missing the point.

As we got back to Daddy's office we nearly collided with two swarthy and muscular men in tight jeans and reflector sunglasses whom Daddy was showing to the door. 'I think we can arrange that for you, Signor Portinari,' one was saying. Daddy coughed discreetly. 'Then there is the other little matter to be taken care of,' he said. 'Leave it to us, Signor

Portinari,' said the other man. 'We'll make him an offer he can't refuse.' They went out of the door and Daddy turned to us. 'Had a good trip?' he asked, shaking our hands. 'See anything that took your fancy? If you're thinking of a little *pied-à-terre* or second home in Babel, we've got some very attractive properties on our books right now. Some excellent investment opportunities around: we're talking an annual return of around 50 per cent and our terms for expatriates are very competitive.'

But my mind was not on investment opportunities. I had been thinking about the bishop's words about the inner cities. 'What about inner-city decay?' I asked. 'Where is it? I didn't see any.' Daddy and his chap looked puzzled. 'Where did you hear about inner-city decay?' they asked. I told them about the morose bishop on the Middle Floors. 'Oh well,' said Daddy, 'that explains it. They're all very behind the times down there.' 'There is no inner-city decay any more,' explained his chap. 'Since the Policy of Urban Renewal and the Movement to Revitalize the Inner Cities, deprivation is a thing of the past. It's true, the City used to be a terrible place. Litter in the streets. Filthy kids everywhere. Not a decent restaurant for miles. Full of unsavoury characters. Couldn't park your Porsche in safety anywhere. But now the whole area has been completely renovated – well, you saw. Business is booming. Property values rising by the minute.'

'The people must have been very grateful,' I said. Daddy's chap looked a bit confused. 'Which people?' he said. 'Well, the ones who live here,' I said. 'The unsavoury ones with the filthy kids.' Daddy's chap continued to look confused, but Daddy burst out laughing. 'They don't live *here*,' he said. 'How could they? They couldn't afford the ground rent on a studio flat, let alone the mortgage on a family house. This area just isn't suitable for them.' 'What is it suitable for?' I asked.

'Investment opportunities,' said Daddy's chap. 'So where are they all? What happened?' 'Relocation,' said Daddy, between gasps of laughter. I didn't understand. Daddy's chap explained. 'They were all relocated under the Bringing Hope Where There Is Despair Act.' 'Where were they relocated to?' I asked. 'Do you know, I'm not absolutely sure,' said Daddy's chap, 'but I believe there was a new development built in the Basement.'

Babel, 26 May, evening

I had succeeded in avoiding the issue of the charter for the duration of the morning, but by lunchtime I was feeling guilty about my negligence, and felt the presence of the document in my pocket as a leaden weight. I determined to devote the afternoon to my mission.

We met the others, who were suffering rather badly from buying fatigue, at Spots (a pointilliste restaurant near the hotel). It was a subdued meal. Hugo and Rosamund were still not on speaking terms. Dorothy and Tracey pointedly ignored each other. Klaus and Rick didn't have the heart for one of their usual sparring matches. Even Miranda's bright and innocuous chatter failed after a while.

After lunch we found ourselves left to our own devices: Richie and her Italian simply disappeared, leaving the rest of us stranded over the caviar and cassata. I can't say I was too sorry. Richie's very pretty, but she's a dead loss as a guide. I never thought I'd find myself missing Virgilia, but at least she was informative. So we all dispersed in different directions. Hugo stumped off gloomily back to the hotel. Rick went to take some photos. Rosamund still had shopping to do. Miranda was a bit lost as Tracey had a rendez-vous with Jason, but eventually decided to go and write postcards on her balcony. Klaus decided to pursue his research on urban renewal among the City backstreets. Which left me alone with Dorothy. I wanted to look for a newspaper office and Dorothy was of the opinion that a turn around the block was good for the digestion, so we set off together down the street, while she told me about her husband who died of heart disease. It runs in his side of the family. Hers is more prone to digestive problems.

We had not gone far before we came to an imposing-looking building. A flight of marble steps ran up to the portico, where a stone slab read: MERDEWAX NEWSPAPERS INC. 'Do you think we could go in?' said Dorothy. 'I've always wanted to see inside a newspaper.' We went up the steps and into a vast echoing marble lobby. The place was completely empty and eerily silent. 'Do you think they've closed down?' said Dorothy. But just then we heard the swish of the lift in its cage and a moment later the doors opened and a young woman in a tailored suit and efficient hairdo stepped out. 'Can I help you?' she said, looking rather suspiciously at our bags and cameras. She continued to look stern as we explained who we were, but at the mention of Richie, she thawed considerably. 'Ah yes,' she said, 'I know her quite well. There's not really much to see here, but come up in the lift with me anyway and I'll show you the office.'

The newspaper offices were nothing like what I expected. I had imagined rooms full of perspiring journalists feverishly tapping away at typewriters while chainsmoking editors yelled out orders, tore up drafts and fretted over deadlines. In Pandora's room, there was nothing but a big machine.
'All journalists have them now,' said Pandora. 'It's called a word processor.' And she showed me its various parts, the textblender, the prose-spicer, the sentence-masher, and the word-mincer. 'I thought journalists didn't mince their words,' I said. 'It's for sensitive government documents,' Pandora

explained and went on to show me the most interesting part of the machine, the additive keys. There were five of them:

PATRIOTISM
SEX (for unusual deviations press SHIFT EXTRA)
ROYAL FAMILY
VIOLENCE
SCANDAL

'They're a wonderful invention,' said Pandora. 'You can't believe how much work they save.' 'How do they work?' I asked. 'Basically, they add that vital interest angle to your piece. Look,' she said and took a raw input item from the feeder. The input item said:

CARROTS TO GO UP BY 2 BAUBELS A KILO

She then keyed in each of the additives in turn and the text was transformed variously as:

BABEL LEADS THE WORLD!
OUR CARROTS ARE THE GREATEST!
Babel's monster carrot crop means that carrot exports have reached their highest level yet. 'Babel is leading the world in this, as in everything else. Our economy is going from strength to strength,' said a triumphant Prime Minister at the opening of the World Carrot Fair. We say, 'Sock it to them, Babel. Show those Krauts and Frogs what carrot production really means!'

LUSCIOUS LINDA CLAIMS CARROTS BEST FOR BONKING
'Everything Mum said was true,' giggled the blonde lovely. 'They do make you see in the dark!'

CARROTS CAUSE RIGHT ROYAL ROW
Palace sources revealed that carrots are a major source of tension in the troubled royal household. His Majesty likes 'em boiled. The Queen prefers 'em raw. Tempers sometimes run high. 'It's not uncommon for a plateful to go whizzing through the air at royal mealtimes,' confided a household aide.

WHAT A WAY TO GO!
COPS CLAIM KEVIN COSHED BY CARROT
A carrot was the murder weapon in last night's fatal attack on Kevin Jones, 19, of Epping. Police are looking for a dark, clean-shaven vegetarian with homicidal tendencies.

STRANGE LOVE HABITS REVEALED AT MILLIONAIRE'S SEX HIDEAWAY
Read our report on page 3!

Dorothy looked intrigued. 'Can you have two at once?' she asked. 'How do you mean?' Pandora asked. 'Well, like Royal Family *and* Sex in the same item.' 'Oh yeah, we often do that. You have to be careful though. Sex and Violence is an obvious one, and so is Sex and Scandal. Patriotism and Violence go well too and Scandal and Royal Family is a winner. But Patriotism and Sex is not really on and Patriotism and Scandal is totally taboo.' 'What do you mean by taboo?' 'Well, you can't press those two keys down together. The machine isn't programmed to do it. It's a new design feature,' she explained. 'Introduced under the Bringing Truth From Error Act.'

'Have all the newspaper offices in Babel been mechanized like this?' I asked. Pandora gave me a funny look. 'All the newspaper offices in Babel are here,' she said, waving her hand around the room. 'Do you mean there's only one newspaper for the whole building?' I asked, stunned. 'But what about all the different languages and cultures?' 'No, no,' said Pandora. 'There are over fifty different daily papers. But they all belong to the Merdewax Group.' 'And what about all the different languages?' I asked. 'Oh, the Processor has a translation chip,' she replied. 'Look, here's a typical Middle Floor translation of Newspiece 2.' And she pressed another button on the keyboard. Luscious Linda and her suggestive carrot disappeared before my eyes as another newspiece assembled itself on the screen.

ORGANICALLY GROWN CARROTS HOLD KEY TO BETTER VISION

Luscious organically-grown carrots have valuable sight-enhancing properties, claims Linda Bonkings, president of the Chipping Sodbury Women Against Chemical Fertilizers group. Research shows that carrots grown in a sympathetic environment contain a higher proportion of vitamins and minerals than chemically fertilized mass-produced carrots. For best results, carrots should be planted at the full-moon and fertilized with goat manure.

'And a Top Floor translation of Newspiece 1 would look like this,' continued Pandora, keying in another code.

CARROT FUTURES MAKE INTERESTING INVESTMENT

A slump in world carrot production, combined with Babel's carrot glut announced yesterday, led to widespread carrot speculation on world stockmarkets today. Trading in carrots has been brisk and at the moment medium-date carrots lead the market, showing gains of up to 300 per cent. Our prediction is that carrot securities could be one of the greatest investments of the twenty-first century.

The demonstration seemed to have come to an end. I felt my moment had come. Rather nervously, I pulled the charter from my pocket. 'I have an item here that might interest you,' I said. Pandora took the charter and glanced through it. 'Well,' she said. 'It doesn't look very eye-catching.' I must have looked disappointed, for she added, 'But let's try.' She fed the document into the raw input feeder. Within seconds the machine disgorged it with a note attached to it. 'Sorry!' it said brightly. 'Regret your product not commercially viable.' Pandora picked it up and handed it back to me with a shrug. 'Why did the machine censor it?' I wanted to know. 'That's not censorship.' Pandora was offended. 'It's market forces. We have complete freedom of the press here in Babel. It's just that your product doesn't have consumer appeal. The machine can't make it fit into any of our categories.'

We thanked Pandora for her kindness in showing us round, and prepared to go. But as we were leaving, a question sprang into my mind. 'But Pandora,' I said, 'the original news item was about the price of carrots.' 'Well?' 'Well, none of the newspieces even mentioned anything about prices.' 'Why should they? That's not what the public wants to hear.'
I was scandalized. 'But that's terrible. That's suppressing information. What about freedom of the press?' 'Rubbish,' said Pandora, firmly. 'What does freedom mean? It means giving people what they want, doesn't it? That's exactly what we're doing.'

Babel, 27 May 1999

I was half disappointed, half relieved at the outcome of yesterday's attempt to publicize the charter. On the one hand the problem of the charter had not gone away; it remained a nagging preoccupation. On the other hand I was mightily relieved not to find myself arrested as a subversive. I don't know what I had expected to happen when Pandora fed the document into the Processor: alarm bell and squadrons of police maybe. But the machine had treated the document with contempt rather than suspicion. I therefore resolved as I was dressing this morning to make one last attempt at publicizing the document.

At breakfast today, Richie and her Italian were nowhere to be found. The lucky chap must be getting a private tour. The rest of us, though, were left to amuse ourselves. Most people were pretty disgruntled at this state of affairs and there was talk of a group letter of complaint to the tour operators. I suppose that at least all this complaining recreated a semblance of group solidarity, but the moans and grumbles quite put me off my breakfast and I decided to go out and get some fresh air. I had no real idea where to go, but thought that perhaps the best place to present a petition was directly to the Government.

I turned down one of the side-streets by the hotel and asked directions from a passer-by. After a few hundred yards I found myself on the bank of a wide muddy brown river. A few minutes' walk through the luxury warehouse conversions and office blocks that lined the banks brought me to a monumental building. People were streaming up the steps and in through the huge oaken doors. As I got nearer I made out letters carved in stone over the entrance. The ornate capitals spelt: NATIONAL WEALTH SERVICE. Also carved into the stone was a crest and a motto, which said:

Cast ye the unprofitable into outer darkness.
Matthew 25, verse 30

I followed the crowd in through the entrance. Immediately inside the doorway was an archway outlined in multi-coloured fairylights. The winking neon letters over the arch spelt out: WEALTH FAIR. I passed through the arch and found myself in a kind of fairground or marketplace. In the background a Big Dipper soared and plunged and an immense Ferris Wheel span giddily round and round to cries of delight and terror. All around me were stalls and booths and the air was full of the cries of vendors and stallholders. For a moment, I thought myself back in the Middle Ages, surrounded by a picturesque bustle of activity and busy commerce. It occurred to me that this might be a good place to look for souvenirs or presents, so I crossed the floor to look at one of the stalls. It was empty. I looked around me. All the other stalls and booths were also bare of goods. Yet all around me was a flurry of buying and selling. Something was obviously changing hands.

I asked one or two of the stallholders nearby what they were selling. Their answers seemed curiously abstract. For a while I didn't understand how you could sell security, buy equity, trade options or deal in risk. It seemed as strange an idea as selling a book without ideas or a painting without a canvas. It began to seem more like a medieval fairground than ever. I wondered if anyone sold pardons or bought indulgences.

As I pressed on through the crowd I had the strangest sensation. It was as if I were passing through a Hall of Mirrors. Everywhere I looked were human forms distorted and mangled out of recognition. Misshapen heads and shrunken legs, hunchbacks and stiltwalkers, swollen bellies and elongated limbs surrounded me on all sides; carbuncles, warts and blebs encrusted foreheads and cheeks; nails sprouted talons; fingers grew twisted and crabbed. But when I looked around there was not a mirror in sight. This was reality, not an image.

I wandered on past a Fat Lady whose pendulous breasts hung nearly to her knees, a Two-Headed Boy, a row of hunchbacked dwarves and a Deformed Head whose enormous mouth eclipsed his nose and eyes, and came to a row of attractions and side-shows.

One of the candy-striped marquees bore the legend: DREAMS OF AVARICE. I lifted the flap and peered inside. Immediately I found myself in an arcade of artificial trees, their leaves and fruit made of gold and silver. As I passed under the branches they curved down and pressed their fruit into my hands. As I closed my hand on the fruit to pluck it, it melted and my hand closed on emptiness. I passed through the arcade and found myself opposite two tents labelled THE MIDAS TOUCH and HOUSE OF CROESUS, and a curious machine called HEIGHTS OF FORTUNE. I decided to try the machine and entered the door, whereupon I found myself in a sort of reverse helter-skelter. I was sliding upwards, dangerously out of control, accelerating unnaturally against the force of gravity. A trapdoor flipped open and I found myself catapulted out into an area of the fairground which seemed populated by soothsayers and quacks, fortune tellers and astrologers. FUTURES MARKET, proclaimed a sign in flashing neon lights. And winking signs over the stalls advertised various kinds of future for sale.

Although I am not naturally superstitious, I wondered whether to have a go, just for the fun of it. I debated what kind of future to buy. I don't know what I was looking for really. Something like Peace and Contentment or Love and Fulfilment would have suited me fine. Health and Energy would have done nicely too. But none of these was on offer.

And none of the futures that were being offered attracted me particularly. International Options sounded exciting, but after this trip, I think I'll have had enough travel for a while. Fixed Interest sounded curiously boring. Debt didn't attract me at all. In the end I decided to settle for Security. A bit boring, maybe, but I'm getting on a bit, and have to think of my retirement.

I approached one of the booths and began to frame my request. 'Excuse me,' I started hesitantly. 'I'm interested in security . . .' The stallholder, who was yelling out a list of figures, appeared not to notice me, but another man, who had been watching from a nearby marquee, came up to me and said, 'If you're interested in security, I have a very attractive proposition for you.'

I followed him to a pink striped marquee, where he held open the flap and beckoned me to enter. We settled ourselves down in plump leather armchairs and he handed me a pile of lavishly bound folders. I started to leaf through them, as the security salesman poured me a glass of whisky and began his sales pitch. 'A confidential assessment of your security requirements,' he began, 'will enable us to offer you the latest in security hardware. Now, if I could begin by asking you a few questions. What, for you, constitutes acceptability? What level of capability do you have already, and what level do you wish to attain?'

These were hard questions. I was not prepared for so much philosophy so early in the morning. 'I suppose an acceptable future for me,' I said slowly, 'would be one where I had a reasonable amount of money and a fairly comfortable house. Not luxurious, just comfortable. And my family nearby. And as to capability, I haven't any great ambitions. I don't want to be a film star or write a novel or anything. But I'd hate to lose my faculties. I'd like to keep on doing things for myself.

I wouldn't want to be dependent on anyone.'

The salesman stared at me, a strange expression on his face. 'Quite,' he said at last, 'but we usually define acceptability in tens of millions and capability in megatons. Would you care to put a figure on your requirements?' This confused me a bit. I hadn't expected human values to be such an exact science. But to humour him I quoted a figure of 10 for acceptability and 20 for capability, hoping that this sounded reasonable. His face cleared. 'Well,' he said, 'I think we can satisfy your requirements. This model, for example, will offer you greatly enhanced capability with very high yield directed energy, while this version can provide assured survival through increased strategic retaliatory capacity.'

I am by nature a mild person and retaliation is usually not in my line, but the idea of enhanced capability and high yield energy in my old age appealed to me, so I chose the first. I was a little disappointed not to be able to take my purchase away with me, as I was curious to see whether it really works or whether it's all a lot of quackery as I suspect, but he promised delivery within six months. We shook hands on the deal, and I walked away. But before I had gone more than a few steps a dreadful thought occurred to me. I had forgotten to ask how much it cost. I turned back, but the tent and the others that surrounded it had mysteriously vanished.

In their place was the entrance to an amusement arcade. The beckoning lights around the entrance spelt out: POLICY PEEPSHOW. I have always loved peepshows, and this one offered the added inducement of postponing the moment when I would have to do something about the charter, so I strayed into the arcade. The first machine I bent over was entitled: A NATION OF SHAREHOLDERS. I turned the handle and a procession of plump and contented burghers filed in front of my eyes. The next said: A NATION

GREAT ONCE AGAIN. Fleets of warships, squadrons of fighter planes, parades of missiles filled the screen as I watched. INDIVIDUAL LIBERTY AND INCREASED CHOICE, said a third. I turned the handle and watched the plump and smiling people shopping. Something had gone wrong with the mechanics of this machine and the film strip was oddly speeded up, so the shoppers were frantically and jerkily grabbing up the goods and slapping down the money. I turned to leave, but as I did, I caught sight of a few neglected and dusty machines towards the rear of the arcade. Bending over the first, I read: COMMUNITY CARE. I turned the creaking handle and was startled by a procession of wild and distraught people, their clothes filthy, their hair unkempt and matted. They wandered like ghosts, moaning and sobbing, among the plump and contented shoppers, who appeared not to notice their presence. YOUTH OPPORTUNITIES, said the next. The handle on this machine had got stuck, so I got no further than the first picture, which showed a number of young people slumped in chairs staring blankly at the flickering screen of a television. A PROPERTY-OWNING DEMOCRACY didn't live up to its promise either. This showed groups of people wrapped in blankets, sheltering under bridges, in dusty tunnels or inside hastily constructed cardboard shacks. But it was the last machine that drew my attention most. ULCER, said the sign, AN ACCEPTABLE LEVEL OF VIOLENCE, which reminded me of something I had seen before. I bent and put my eye to the peephole but recoiled almost immediately in shock. My eye was met by a great kaleidoscope of whirling images, which erupted from a central vortex as if from a gigantic explosion. Tangles of barbed wire sprayed out from the centre, knotting and retwisting themselves in a huge circular pattern of clumps and loops. These gave way to multiple images of guns and bayonets which mirrored and reduplicated themselves in whirling symmetry before dissolving into spinning patterns of severed and bleeding limbs, mouths open in soundless gapes of pain, the staring eyes of the dead and the agonized eyes of the living, all consumed in turn by a ball of fire which leapt from the centre and disintegrated into a thousand identical licking flames. At the centre of this grotesque kaleidoscope was what seemed like a great red rose of living flesh, a giant rodent ulcer that ceaselessly devoured itself and spewed out these images of hate and sorrow.

Shaken, I turned to go, and left the arcade. Outside, the stalls and booths had vanished and I found myself on the landing of an elaborate and sweeping stairway. The stairs curved up to a wide landing where I saw a blue painted door with a glass window set in it. Large white letters painted on the door said: RULES DEPARTMENT. Underneath an official looking but rather tattered document was tacked to the door. It said:

There are two rules:

1. Unto everyone that hath, shall be given.
2. From him that hath not, shall be taken away.

Matthew 25, verse 29

I peered through the glass pane into the room. The gloomy cavernous interior was filled with row after row of desks at which sat row after row of clerks, scribbling feverishly, sucking their pens reflectively or sifting through mounds of paper with inkstained fingers. I was wondering whether this was the right place to present a petition, when a crisp-looking lady in a tailored suit clattered briskly down the stairs from the floor above. 'Oh, there you are,' she said, coming up to me and thrusting a sheaf of documents into my hand. 'Quickly now, take these to section 438. And bring me the draft of memo 397, would you.' And before I had time to protest or explain, she turned and bustled back up the stairs, the click of her high heels resounding down the stairwell and echoing along the empty corridor.

I looked at the documents in my hand. They were headed, 'Resolution 5476A: Nuclear Power – a smoke-free fuel for a cleaner Babel.' Taking a deep breath, I pushed open the door and went in. I needn't have been afraid. No one looked up. Heads bent, they went on scribbling and shuffling or stared vacantly into the middle distance. I stepped over to one of the desks and enquired timidly of the girl sitting there, 'Excuse me, could you tell me how to get to section 438 please?' Without looking up, she replied, 'Straight on through Image Enhancement and Media Profile, first left, go right through Figures Massage, left again then second right after Face-saving and Cover-ups, and you'll come to Disguises and Whitewash.' It seemed I had come to a beauty salon.

I made my way through the rows of desks and eventually, after getting hopelessly lost in the Figures Massage department and an unscheduled detour through Retouching and Glossing Over, I arrived at 438 and handed over my document. 'And could I have memo 397?' I asked the clerk. 'Oh, that's back in Whitewash,' she replied. 'Senior Citizens' Health and Welfare section.' Something about this sounded familiar, and when I tracked down the memo and began to read it as I made my way back to the door, I realized where I had seen something similar.

'NIGHTCAPS: A GOVERNMENT OF BABEL DOCUMENT,' it read, and continued:

> It has come to the attention of the Babel government that a certain proportion of Senior Citizens have resorted to the

use of nightcaps at bedtime, perhaps in the erroneous belief that this will raise their body temperature. This belief is scientifically incorrect. A number of studies have shown that nightcaps not only lower body temperature, but are generally deleterious to health. The Babel government is naturally concerned about the health of its Senior Citizens, and to this effect a number of measures have been suggested:

1. The tax on alcohol should be raised forthwith, to discourage this unhealthy habit.
2. Senior Citizens should be encouraged to knit, instead of drink, nightcaps. This would have the dual effect of providing them with an interesting and productive occupation to take their minds off alcohol, and of keeping them warm at night.
3. Leftover wool scraps for nightcaps could be collected under the I AM GENEROUS scheme.

This was the neatly typed version. The original draft was somewhat different. It was headed, 'June Budget: Fiscal Policy.' 'Fuel costs to go up by 25 per cent,' it read.

My errand here completed, I wondered if there was a department who would tell me what to do with my charter. I looked at the signs to the various departments. None of them sounded very promising. In the end I took the envelope out of my pocket and showed it to the girl at the nearest desk. 'Can you tell me where I should go with this?' I said. She took a cursory glance at it. 'I don't understand the language,' she said. 'What is it?' 'I think it's some kind of protest,' I said. 'Protest?' she said, uncomprehendingly. 'Complaint, then. Do you have a department that deals with complaints?' 'Oh, I don't know,' she said dubiously. 'I've never ever seen one before. But then I'm new here. Ask Ken. He's been here nearly twenty years.' A portly old gentleman who must have been near retirement age leant over and scrutinized the letter. 'Oh yes,' he said. 'I do dimly recall seeing that sort of thing before, but I haven't seen anything like that for the last ten years. There's no one here who can translate that sort of stuff any more.' 'What shall I do with it?' I asked. 'Let me see,' he said, frowning, as he tried to recollect. 'I think we used to send out one of these.' He fumbled around in his desk drawer and unearthed a small card which he handed to me. The card said, 'Your communication is being dealt with.' 'And then,' he continued, 'we used to put the document in one of the files in section M.' I thanked him and turned to go, colliding as I did so with a small balding man who was standing right behind me, an anxious expression behind his misty pebble lenses.

It took me some time to find my way through the maze, but eventually I reached section M. There was only one file on the very top shelf, I reached for it and brought it down amid a shower of dust and cobwebs. It was nearly empty. Inside were two or three yellowing and faded documents. I looked at the titles at the top. CHARTER 88, said the first. The second said: CHARTER 89. I didn't look at the third. Instead, I brushed off the dust and tried to read the faded letters on the cover. They read: PENDING. I stood and considered my position. It didn't seem a very hopeful destination for the document entrusted to my care. On the other hand, I was anxious to complete my quest: a mission I was convinced had been a misunderstanding from start to finish. I had carried out their instructions to the best of my ability. Was it my fault if this was the way the system worked? In the end I decided to give it one last try and take it to a higher authority. I would ask the woman who had sent me into the Rules Department. She had an air of brisk efficiency. Perhaps she would help me. I replaced the file, put the document in my pocket and turned to go, almost knocking over a plumpish balding man who was squinting up at the file through misty pebble lenses.

I regained the door, and wondered where to find the lady of the crisp suit and clicking heels. I went up the stairs to the next floor and found myself in a maze of corridors. Standing perplexed at the head of the stairs wondering which way to go, I heard a familiar sound echoing from the corridor on my right. I followed the sound down the corridor, and turned the corner in time to see a neatly tailored suit disappearing into a door at the far end. I followed her and opened the door. I found myself at the back of a huge hall which had rows of tiered seats rising in two banks from a central well. The right-hand bank was full of people all earnestly discussing something, murmuring agreement and turning round to congratulate each other. The left-hand bank of seats was empty. The crisp lady had settled herself into a seat at the back of the hall. She had taken out a notepad and appeared to be listening intently and making notes on the discussion.

I sat down next to her and passed her the memo. 'Thank you,' she said. Then, looking at me, 'Who are you?' I explained, while below us the discussion went on and the murmurs of assent rose and fell. When I had finished, she looked distinctly dubious. 'I'm not sure you should be here,' she said. 'It seems to be highly irregular to me.' 'Oh, but I'm finding it absolutely fascinating,' I assured her earnestly. 'You have a wonderful system here in Babel.' She seemed mollified. 'Well, since you are here,' she said, grudgingly, 'I suppose you might as well stay, though we don't usually take tour groups round the government building.' 'Is this the Government?' I asked, looking round eagerly. The room was very grand. On one wall was a huge portrait. Opposite it hung an illuminated text which read:

Blessed are the rich, for they shall inherit the family estate;
Blessed are the wealth-makers, for they shall make the nation great;
Blessed are the piece-workers, for they lower production costs;
Blessed are they that hunger and thirst after profit, for they shall be filled.

I took this in and turned back to my companion, who was writing in her notebook. 'Who are you?' I asked. 'Are you a member of the Government?' 'I'm a Backbencher,' she said, writing away. 'Do you mind if I ask a few questions?' 'Fire away,' she said, 'I'll do my best.' 'Well, the memo I brought you from the Health section made me think about health in Babel. Where are the hospitals? Is there a special floor for them?' 'Oh no,' she said. 'Each floor has its own health system. As you've probably realized, people in Babel have very different lifemodes, so we try to accommodate for that in our hospital facilities.' 'How do you mean?' 'Well, for a start, there are concept-related diseases. Inhabitants of the Top Floor tend to suffer from quite different complaints from Basementdwellers, for example.' 'What do you mean?' I asked. 'Well, typical Top Floor diseases are heart attacks, gout, liver failure or apoplexy.' 'What about Basement diseases?' 'Oh, rickets, scurvy, that kind of thing. And then, we make other adjustments. For example, such things as space, speed, efficiency and privacy are Top Floor-related lifemodes, whereas on the Ground Floor their comfort-desirability and human-intimacy thresholds are lower, so we make the necessary concessions to reduce the sensation of mode-displacement. You need to feel at home when you're ill. And in the Basement, queuing is an old folk custom, so they relate naturally to waiting lists. So we do our best to provide for that too.' 'It sounds very well worked out,' I said. 'Yes,' she said comfortably, 'we have things very well worked out here in general. Was there anything else you wanted to know about?'

'Yes,' I said. 'I've been wondering about languages in Babel. The system doesn't seem logical to me.' She frowned. Small lines of impatience began to appear round her mouth. 'The system is absolutely logical,' she said. 'What in particular has been bothering you?' 'Well, the Resolution that I delivered for you about nuclear power and the greenhouse effect . . .' 'Yes?' she said suspiciously. 'It seemed to me that it was in the same language – used the same vocabulary – as the language I heard on the Middle Floors, in the Ecology chapel.' 'Oh no,' she said firmly, 'you're quite mistaken there. The words may look the same. They may sound the same. But they have a completely different meaning up here.'

I realized the truth of what she said. After all it was not uncommon to find words that looked or sounded the same in different languages, but which were completely unrelated. I had another query though. 'And another thing,' I began, 'it seems to me that, whereas on the other floors the people in the same concept-modules all spoke the same language, it seems to me that up here I've heard a lot of different languages.' She cut me short. 'Now you're quite wrong there,' she said. 'Up here we all speak the same language.' And she went back to writing on her pad.

We sat in silence for some minutes, while the Backbencher took notes and I looked around the huge hall and tried to follow the discussion.'What are they doing?' I asked eventually. 'Debating the Light Privatization Bill,' she said, scribbling furiously on her pad. 'Light Privatization?' 'Yes,' she said, still scribbling. 'Funny, isn't it, that they've only just come round to it.' 'What do you mean?' I asked. 'Well, that an important natural commodity like light has been unexploited for so long. People just took it for granted. Used it without paying. Strange isn't it? It's rather like thinking just because you were born in a country you have a right to some of its land, or can drink its water for free.' 'So who does light belong to?' I asked. 'To the Government at the moment,' said the Backbencher, 'but they're in the process of selling it off to Natural Facilities Ltd. They already own water and gas.' 'And everyone will have to pay for light?' I couldn't imagine how it would work. 'That's right,' said the Backbencher, chewing her pencil reflectively. 'Everyone will pay for the light they use.' 'But *how*?' I still couldn't understand how light could be bought. 'Well, I expect it'll be rather like water and gas,' said the Backbencher. 'Everyone will have a light meter.'

I thought I understood. 'So some people, like those who live in big houses, or have offices with lots of windows, will have to pay more?' 'That's what they're debating at the moment,' said the Backbencher. 'But I don't think it'll turn out exactly like that. That would be unfair victimization of homeowners and people who have built up their own businesses, and this government is very careful to protect minority rights. So I think there'll be some exclusion clauses and special business tariffs.' 'Who'll pay light charges then?' 'I'm not exactly sure,' said the Backbencher, flipping her notebook shut and preparing to leave, 'but most people seem to be in favour of making the burden of the charges fall on those who overuse or abuse the light facility.' That seemed quite fair to me. 'Such as?' 'Well, people who work or live outside: builders, labourers, fruit pickers, for example. And the light abusers like tramps and beggars. Gipsies. Hippy Convoys. That sort of thing.'

She packed up her things and we moved off down the corridor. 'I wonder they haven't privatized air,' I said to myself. The Backbencher overheard me. 'Air's too important to privatize,' she said. 'It might get into the wrong hands. So the Government took over total air control. The Air Protection Act 1990. But there is an Air Tax.' 'What do they tax – the air people have in their houses or what?' 'It used to be like that,' said the Backbencher, 'before the Liberation of the Ratepayer. Then there was a system whereby people used to be taxed on the amount of air they had inside their houses. So if you had a small house you paid less Air Tax, and if you had a big house you paid more Air Tax. But then the Government realized that the system was terribly unfair, because people weren't necessarily *using* all the air inside their houses. And you'd get ridiculous anomalies. You could get, for example, a small house paying a very low rate of Air Tax, but there might be eight people living in there, using vast quantities of air. Or you might get a huge house with only one or two people in it, using very limited amounts of air. And they were having to foot an enormous Air Tax bill, when the air in some of those rooms probably hadn't been used for centuries.'

'So now what do they tax?' 'The air actually used, of course. Air Tax is worked out on a per capita breath rate for every household. A much fairer way of doing it. And it allowed the Government to take extra measures to control air pollution. Clean Air Act 1992.' 'Do you mean controls on smoke?' 'Not exactly, no. But a lot of people were using air for a variety of undesirable and harmful activities.' 'Such as?' 'Making speeches. Leaking documents. Telling secrets. Things like that.' 'So were they banned?' The Backbencher was shocked. 'Goodness me, no,' she said. 'We have complete freedom of speech in Babel. The Government just placed certain restrictions on air pollution.' 'So anyone can say anything they want?' 'That's right,' said the Backbencher, happily. 'You just can't use air to say it in.'

This seemed like a good moment to hand over the petition. But something held me back, and instead of doing so at once, I prudently enquired, 'What is Babel policy on dissent?' It was the Backbencher's turn to look puzzled. 'Dissent?' she queried. 'Yes. What happens to dissidents in Babel?' She looked blankly at me. 'Dissidents?' 'People who don't agree.' She still looked blank. 'But how could they not agree? The concept of dissent no longer exists. We recognize that everyone has a right to their own linguistic mode, and since the Sealed Concept Module policy, everyone is with like-minded people so there is no cause for dissent. We even have special concept modules for those whose verbal mode is defined by disagreement, like terrorists or university lecturers. There they can be with their own kind and argue happily amongst themselves without infringing on anyone else's opinion-field. We have eliminated the possibility of dissent. That's what the Bringing Harmony Where There Was Discord policy is all about.' But something still troubled me. 'But what about people who think that everyone should be in the same concept module?' 'Like Marxists, you mean? The same goes for them as for anyone else. It's a belief like any other. They have their own concept module. Next door to Terrorists.'

I wasn't satisfied. Something still gnawed at me. 'But what about,' I brought out at length, 'people who don't agree with the concept of concept modules?' The Backbencher looked uneasy. 'I don't follow you,' she said. I wasn't sure that I was following my own train of thought too well. Hesitantly, I tried to formulate what I meant. 'People who . . . who think there shouldn't be separate modules. I don't mean people who think everyone should think the same thing or that there's only one right way of thinking, but people who think that there should be discussion and disagreement, that all kinds of people with different languages and beliefs should be able to mix freely and share . . .' The Backbencher cut me short. 'Such persons do not exist,' she said crisply. 'If they did they would be a threat to the fabric of a harmonious society. They would be causing a serious breach of the peace and would be dealt with under the Public Order and Prevention of Discord Act.'

We had now reached the stairs, and here the Backbencher said goodbye, a little icily, and set off for the Members' Bar. I wondered what to do next. My quest was still unfulfilled. Somehow she hadn't seemed the right person to entrust with the document I carried.

Then a figure emerged from the shadows at the end of the corridor. 'Who are you?' I asked, a little sharply. He had made me jump. Then I recognized him. It was the small man with the anxious expression whom I had so nearly knocked over in the Rules Department. He looked around nervously. 'I'm a Wet,' he whispered, proffering a limp handshake. 'I couldn't help overhearing your conversation. Can we talk?' 'Delighted,' I said. 'What about? About dissent?' 'Not here,' he whispered urgently, looking over his shoulder. 'Not now. I'll meet you outside in the street in about ten minutes.'

I went out and loitered around on the street corner outside the Wealth Service, and in a few minutes the Wet came scurrying down the steps of the building. He passed me without speaking, but winked furtively, and indicated with an almost imperceptible movement of his head that I should follow him. I walked a discreet distance behind, pretending to look around and admire the buildings, as he took me down a street, across a road, past a shopping arcade and finally down a small alley, and into a deserted building.

We're safe here,' he said, with a sigh of relief, dropping into one of a row of plush covered seats and motioning to me to do the same. 'What is this place?' I asked, looking round the gloomy hall. 'It used to be a theatre. It was the last one to close, in fact,' he said. 'And now they're going to turn it into a luxury Jacuzzi complex.' 'What do you mean by "safe"?' I asked. 'And why did you bring me here?' 'As I told you, I'm a Wet,' he said. 'There aren't many of us left. I only survived by keeping my mouth shut and going underground. Otherwise I might have ended up like the others.' 'Where *did* the others end up?' I asked. 'Out on their noses, usually,' said the Underground Wet. 'Some were dried out, of course. But some ended up in the Northern Ireland section of the Rules Department or drafting quotas for EEC chicken feed imports. Some were even sent to the SDP. Never came back from there of course.' He sighed, deeply and sadly. 'I still don't understand,' I said. 'What *are* Wets? Why do they have to live underground? And what do you want to talk to me about?' The Underground Wet leant confidentially towards me, 'I overheard what you said about dissent,' he said earnestly. 'And it's true. There are some of us around who don't believe in concept modules.'

Gradually, the truth sank in. I was talking to another dissident. What did I do to attract them? But the Wet was still in full flow. 'I belong to ARCH,' he was saying. 'Association for Rediscovery of our Common Humanity. It's a banned organization, of course. Used to be quite a big concern. Writers, actors, poets, playwrights, journalists, Arts Council administrators all belonged. You even got a few modern artists in there. The Church was right behind us and we even had a royal patron.' 'What happened to all your members?' I asked. The Wet sighed. A tear trickled down his nose. 'They got picked off, one by one,' he said. 'Some got censored. Others had their funds cut off. Most ended up in the Basement.' 'What about the royal patron?' I asked, curiously. 'Did he end up in the Basement too?' 'No. You can't send a monarch there even if he is unemployed. They got him under the Clean Air Act, though. He made one speech too many. Now he's virtually denied airspace. Christmas speeches all cancelled, and they've banned him from laying any more foundation stones in case he sounds off about modern architecture or inner cities again. Kept in the palace. Only allowed out for State Openings and at Media Viewing Time.' He sniffed audibly and blinked back another tear.

'And what are the ideals of your society?' I asked, proffering a handkerchief. 'What do you believe in?' The Wet blew his nose and continued, 'We don't believe in linguistic segregation for a start,' he said. 'We're working for a multi-faceted, culturally-diversified, ideologically-varied society, where people no longer fear disagreement, but which nevertheless functions as a cohesive whole through the rediscovery of our universal emotions, the reactivation of compassion, and the re-establishment of a common vocabulary.' It sounded like heady stuff. 'Here,' he said, delving into his pocket, 'perhaps you'd like to read some of our literature.' He had cheered up considerably. I looked at the leaflets and posters he had given me. One poster read: SEGREGATION EQUALS STULTIFICATION. Another was headed: LANGUAGE IS ONLY SKIN-DEEP.

The title of one pamphlet was 'Towards a Common Language'. Others were called 'What is Compassion? – Your questions answered' and 'Harmony can be Boring'. 'End linguistic stagnation now!' exhorted this last one, 'Explore some new language possibilities! Have a row with your wife tonight!' 'Rather subversive stuff, I'm afraid,' said the Wet, with a half embarrassed chuckle, when he saw me looking at this last one. 'Written by one of our extremists. I'm not sure I'd go that far myself.'

'What would you like me to do?' I asked. 'Did you ask me here to help you?' 'Well,' he said cautiously, 'that depends on you. Are you in sympathy with the aims of our organization?' 'The compassion part sounds OK,' I replied, equally cautiously, 'but I'm not so sure about the universal emotions bit.' He looked a little crestfallen, so I added hurriedly, 'but in any case I support your right to disagree. I don't think anyone should be censored or have their funds cut off. And I thought the Basement was a terrible place.'

The Wet brightened up. 'I and my organization would be eternally grateful to you if you were willing to complete a small mission for us,' he said. I must have looked alarmed, for he went on consolingly, 'No, no, don't worry, we wouldn't ask you to do anything dangerous. We just want you to take a small parcel out of the country for us.' 'What does it contain?' I asked suspiciously. Again he hurried to reassure me, 'Nothing dangerous at all,' he said. 'Just a few books.' 'Books?' 'Yes. As you may have gathered, literature was declared obsolete under the Bringing Truth From Error Act, and after the Dissolution of the Libelries it was hard to find a pair of hard covers with any words between them at all. A few of us hung onto our old books, but since the Bringing Faith From Doubt Act, doubt was made illegal, and possessing a book was declared an act of doubt. So it's getting really dangerous to keep books here in Babel.' 'So you want me to smuggle some books out for you?' 'If you would, yes. I'll give you a contact address to hand them on to when you're out of the country. Someone who'll keep them safe till happier times come and we're free to print things again. Otherwise they risk getting lost for good. And by the way,' he added, 'you'd better take that charter out with you too.' I protested that my mission was to publicize it on the Top Floor. He shook his head, smiling as if at a child or a simpleton. 'It won't do any good,' he said. 'They'll only put it in the PENDING file or pretend it was never delivered and no one will ever see it again. No, the only thing is to take it out: publish it somewhere else.' I couldn't see any reasonable objection to this proposal. It seemed a good way out of my dilemma.

So I've agreed to meet the Underground Wet and another ARCH agent here before breakfast tomorrow for the handover of the books.

Seat 37C, Flight BA372, 28 May 1999

I awoke early this morning from a strange and vivid dream. I had found myself in a dark and eerily silent corridor. I did not know where I was and there was no one about to help me. Suddenly I noticed in the shadows, at the end of the corridor, a narrow wrought-iron spiral staircase, twisting up and up, apparently into nowhere. I decided to see where it led. The climb seemed endless, and I was about to give up, when the steps ended abruptly against what seemed to be the ceiling of the corridor. I felt around with my hands and encountered a kind of wooden panel or trapdoor. I gave it a push and it yielded to my pressure. Suddenly the staircase and the whole corridor below it was illuminated with a white and dazzling light. Half-blinded, I pulled myself up through the trapdoor onto the roof of the building and, blinking hard, gazed around me at what I saw. Light came towards me in shining waves and I felt I was drowning in the brilliant flood which engulfed me. As my eyes grew more accustomed to the brilliance, a strange vision seemed to crystallize out of the heart of the light. At first it looked like a huge white rose; its snowy petals glimmering and shining with pure white light. Then I realized what it was. It was the council chamber I had sat in yesterday: its tiered rows of seats forming the multiple petals of the rose. Bathed in the unearthly radiance of the light, it had become transfigured into a celestial vision. Even the occupants of the seats, the members who had been debating so earnestly yesterday, looked transformed: their garments radiant, their faces shining with an angelic light. Suddenly my eyes were drawn to a figure who appeared at the outermost edge of the rose. She advanced to one of the seats, a golden throne forming one of the outer petals of the rose, but as she took her place and opened her mouth to speak, the vision faded and I awoke to the chill half-light of early dawn in my hotel room. I had recognized her face though. It was the face from the enormous portrait that hung in the council chamber.

For a while I lay in bed, trying to retrace all the details of my dream and marvelling at the tricks my subconscious had played with the previous day's events. I wondered if the dream had a meaning. How should I interpret the light, the rose? Then I realized with a start that it was getting late and that I had an appointment to keep before breakfast.

I got up quickly and dressed and packed my suitcase. As I folded my clothes, I came across a small crumpled piece of paper. I smoothed it out and read once again the computer's cryptic message. This did not clarify anything. I now felt more puzzled than ever. Did the encoded message mean that I was to take the charter to the Lady of the Rose? But surely she was just a creation of my dream. I am a rational person and I do not as a rule believe in visions, supernatural dreams or divine messages. I refused to entertain the idea that my dream was sent to tell me something: that seemed too preposterous. In the end I rationalized the Lady and her appearance to me as I slept as another fragment of the last few days' events that my subconscious had fitted into its crazy jigsaw puzzle of a dream.

Nevertheless, I still felt slightly uneasy as I took the lift down to the marble lobby of the hotel. The clerk at the reception desk looked a little surprised to see me up and about so early, but I told him that it was my habit to take a brisk walk before breakfast, and he seemed satisfied. I had a bad moment when I took a wrong turning down one of the side-streets near the Wealth Service, but doubled back, and eventually recognized the street with the theatre. I broke into a run. I was twenty minutes late. Suppose they had given up and gone.

But when I pushed open the auditorium door, the two ARCH-Wets were waiting anxiously. We only had time for a brief consultation, during which they handed me a small key labelled 217, and told me that the parcel would be in the left-luggage lockers at the liftport. I was to check in my baggage first, but retain one piece of hand-baggage. Then, under some pretext or other, I was to leave the tour group, retrieve the parcel from the locker and keep it in my hand-baggage. 'But what if they find it at Customs?' I asked. 'They won't search you,' said the Underground Wet. 'They're more interested in what comes in than what goes out. And in any case we've disguised the books as Babel tourguides and handbooks. They won't look twice at those.' We shook hands and began to say goodbye. But my dream this morning was still preying on my mind, and on an impulse I asked the Wets whether I could get to the Roof to deliver the charter. They were scandalized. 'No one is allowed up there,' they said. 'The official entrance is from the National Wealth Service but it's heavily guarded. No one knows what goes on up there any more. We just carry out the orders. Take our word for it,' they said, 'the best thing you could do with that charter is to take it out of the country as fast as possible.' We shook hands solemnly, I wished them good luck and we left the building by separate entrances.

The walk back to the hotel passed without incident, and on my return, I found the breakfast room in an excited uproar. Richie and her Italian were still nowhere to be found and bets were being laid on whether he would be joining us for the flight back or not. John the Baptist, on the other hand, had rematerialized, apparently unchanged by his group encounters.

At the liftport I checked in my luggage, and, my heart beating fast, made an excuse to leave the group. Our lift, I saw as I crossed the concourse, was delayed by forty minutes. To reach the left-luggage lockers I had to go out of the main entrance and in again by a side entrance, a hundred yards or so away, and it was as I was walking down the corridor towards this entrance that a strange thing happened. Looking ahead of me, in the half-shadows at the end of the corridor, I saw a twisting staircase, exactly like the one in my dream. A shiver ran down my spine and my heart began to pound. I felt in the grip of something uncanny. But, as you know, I'm not naturally superstitious, and I quickly rationalized this by explaining to myself that of course I must have seen the staircase out of the corner of my eye when we left the liftport on our arrival on the Top Floor three days ago. By some mysterious process, my subconscious had stored it away, and it had resurfaced in my dream. Fortified with this comfortable theory, I no longer felt the eerie chill of the supernatural, but instead experienced an overpowering compulsion to climb the staircase and see what was on the Roof. 'Just a peep,' I promised myself, looking at my watch. 'After all, there's an hour and a half before the lift leaves.' So I started to climb the stairs.

To my surprise, the climb was over quite quickly, but to my far greater surprise, the stairway ended, exactly as my dream had foretold it would, in a trapdoor in the ceiling. My heart started to thump again, and my fingers seemed to have turned to ice. But I was committed now. I had to see what was beyond the trapdoor. Eyes half-closed, I pushed at the door, preparing myself for the blinding rush of light. But none came. I looked up into an area of darkness. I could see nothing, hear nothing. Gritting my teeth, I reached for the edges of the trap and pulled myself up into the void above me.

I looked around me. It was not as pitch black as it had seemed from below, and as my eyes grew accustomed to the gloom, I made out strange twilight shapes, which gradually took form as bulging sacks, jars, bottles, packets. I was in some kind of storeroom. I could now hear the muffled sound of voices and was able to distinguish a door at the far end of the room. From beneath it came the glimmer of light that illumined the room, and from beyond it came the sound of the voices. I moved cautiously towards it and listened. A voice, harsh and shrill, was saying, 'How many times do I have to tell you that we don't give credit here? If you want something you have to pay for it. We've no time for scroungers here. Go and do a decent day's work, like the rest of us.' Mystified, I opened the door a crack and peered out.

The scene I saw before me transported me back in time a century or more. It was like getting a glimpse into the world behind an old painting or as if an ancient photo had suddenly sprung into life. I was looking into a small, sombre, but neatly-kept shop. Bottles, jars and packets were arranged in tidy rows on the shelves, sacks of flour, tea and coffee stood in one corner. The floor was swept clean and a scrubbed wooden counter ran across the shop from left to right. Across this counter a woman was leaning. She wore a long dark silk dress with a bustle and lace stole, and her head was covered with a bonnet trimmed with flowers. She was bending across the counter to shout at another woman, barefoot, in filthy tattered clothes, who held a crying baby in her arms and led a ragged snot-nosed brat by the hand. The shrill voice went on and on; the face beneath the bonnet was distorted with distaste and dislike.

As I watched, a man came forward from behind the counter and, roughly seizing the beggarwoman, bundled her out of the shop. The woman behind the counter stood back, smoothing down her dress with her hands and turned to greet her next customer, a stout ruby-faced gentleman with waistcoat, top-hat and walking stick. Bending a beaming face on him, she said, 'So sorry about that. Unfortunate incident. These parasites think they can take advantage of decent working folk. Never done a day's work in their lives, some of them.' 'Quite,' said the stout gentleman, his side-whiskers twitching, 'these layabouts must be taught a lesson. A pound of coffee, please.' 'Certainly, Mr Puffwig,' replied the shopkeeper, her countenance now transformed by smiles. 'Shall I charge it to your account?' 'If you would. And a jar of mustard, too, please.'

I had seen enough. I silently closed the door and retraced my steps across the storeroom. I climbed back down the stairway, pondering the significance of what I had seen. As I reached the bottom, one fact sorted itself out from the rest and danced around in my head. The face I had seen in the shop, so distorted by anger and disgust, was the face in my dream, the face of the Lady of the Rose, the face from the giant portrait.

But I had no time to reflect on this. As I started off towards the left-luggage lockers, I could hear my lift being called in the concourse. I raced along the corridor, found my locker, turned the key and grabbed the bulky parcel that I found there. Thrusting it into my cabin bag, I ran back to the concourse and rejoined the others at the passport control. Luckily they were all so preoccupied with speculating on our absconded Italian that they had not even noticed my absence. I joined up with Dorothy, Hugo and Rosamund and we went through the passport and customs formalities together and caught the high security lift to the airport where our plane was waiting.

Once on the plane, I settled into my seat, and tucked the books carefully in beside me so that they were hidden from view. Behind me I heard Rick talking to one of the transit passengers from New York. 'Ever been to Babel?' he was saying. 'You should go there sometime. It's a really neat place. Why, when I was on the Top Floor . . .' Of course. Future tour groups would hear about Babel, as we had heard about Guinea and Peru. I wondered what the others were doing, but I didn't need to ask the question. I knew. Klaus would be drowning the person next to him in a recital of facts. Hugo and Rosamund, their quarrel made up, would be holding hands and gazing into each other's eyes, oblivious to the rest of the world. Tracey would have found the most attractive man on the plane and seated herself next to him. Miranda would be staring dreamily out of the window. Dorothy's feet would be swollen due to the altitude. Johnny . . . what did Johnny do between Experiences? I looked over my shoulder, craning my neck. Johnny was sitting in the lotus position, a faraway smile on his face, ignoring the stewardess who was telling him to fasten his seat belt. Travel as romantic backdrop or sexual playground, as attribute of the personality or escape from self, as something to be consumed, like a box of chocolates, or hoarded greedily, added to your store of possessions: each had taken from Babel exactly what they had come to find. Well, was I any different? I *did* feel changed, but not in the way you are supposed to be changed by travel: I felt somehow diminished by the experience: angrier, less trusting, less hopeful.

When the plane had taken off, my whisky had been served, and we had left Babel airspace, I succumbed to curiosity and opened my parcel. There were four or five books, all disguised in glossy new jackets bearing titles like *The Pocket Guide to Babel* or *A Short Guide to the World's Tallest Country*.

Cautiously, I opened one of the books. I don't know what I expected. The latest in dissident writing, I suppose. But this book was very old. The spine was crumbling, and the yellowing pages were spilling out from the covers. The sweet musty odour of old paper rose to my nostrils. The book was terribly defaced. An unknown hand had been through with a blue pencil, scoring out passages, and adding comments in the margin. The page where I had opened the book was cross-hatched with lines and deletions, and one passage had been heavily underscored. The blue pencilled comment in the margin read: 'ANTI-GOVERNMENT BIAS!!' I looked down at the passage and began to read:

> once or twice
> I was about to speak and tell him plainly
> The selfsame sun that shines upon his court
> Hides not his visage from our cottage, but
> Looks on alike.

I closed the book and turned to stare out of the window. My mind was cluttered with images: the fairground, the University, the gateway to the Basement. The images shifted and jostled with each other until finally one rose to the surface, dominating the others: the vision of the Lady of the Rose, the petals of that illusory rose fading, withering and falling away till at the heart of the rose nothing was left but the small dark shop. Looking out through the dimpled panes of the shop window, I saw faces pressed to the glass looking in, staring with hopeless and with empty eyes. And behind them, beyond them, stretching into the distance, the vast multitude of the destitute, the barefoot, the old, the young, the crippled, the ragged, the homeless, the broken, the helpless.

I closed my eyes and wept.